BASIL THOMSON
WHO KILLED STELLA POMEROY

SIR BASIL HOME THOMSON (1861-1939) was educated at Eton and New College Oxford. After spending a year farming in Iowa, he married in 1889 and worked for the Foreign Service. This included a stint working alongside the Prime Minister of Tonga (according to some accounts, he *was* the Prime Minister of Tonga) in the 1890s followed by a return to the Civil Service and a period as Governor of Dartmoor Prison. He was Assistant Commissioner to the Metropolitan Police from 1913 to 1919, after which he moved into Intelligence. He was knighted in 1919 and received other honours from Europe and Japan, but his public career came to an end when he was arrested for committing an act of indecency in Hyde Park in 1925 – an incident much debated and disputed.

His eight crime novels featuring series character Inspector Richardson were written in the 1930's and received great praise from Dorothy L. Sayers among others. He also wrote biographical and criminological works.

Also by Basil Thomson

Richardson's First Case
Richardson Scores Again
The Case of Naomi Clynes
The Case of the Dead Diplomat
The Dartmoor Enigma
The Milliner's Hat Mystery
A Murder is Arranged

BASIL THOMSON

WHO KILLED STELLA POMEROY?

With an introduction by
Martin Edwards

DEAN STREET PRESS

Published by Dean Street Press 2016

First published in 1936 by Eldon Press as
Death in the Bathroom

Cover by DSP

Introduction © Martin Edwards 2016

ISBN 978 1 911095 77 4

www.deanstreetpress.co.uk

Introduction

SIR BASIL THOMSON's stranger-than-fiction life was packed so full of incident that one can understand why his work as a crime novelist has been rather overlooked. This was a man whose CV included spells as a colonial administrator, prison governor, intelligence officer, and Assistant Commissioner at Scotland Yard. Among much else, he worked alongside the Prime Minister of Tonga (according to some accounts, he *was* the Prime Minister of Tonga), interrogated Mata Hari and Roger Casement (although not at the same time), and was sensationally convicted of an offence of indecency committed in Hyde Park. More than three-quarters of a century after his death, he deserves to be recognised for the contribution he made to developing the police procedural, a form of detective fiction that has enjoyed lasting popularity.

Basil Home Thomson was born in 1861 – the following year his father became Archbishop of York – and was educated at Eton before going up to New College. He left Oxford after a couple of terms, apparently as a result of suffering depression, and joined the Colonial Service. Assigned to Fiji, he became a stipendiary magistrate before moving to Tonga. Returning to England in 1893, he published *South Sea Yarns*, which is among the 22 books written by him which are listed in Allen J. Hubin's comprehensive bibliography of crime fiction (although in some cases, the criminous content was limited).

Thomson was called to the Bar, but opted to become deputy governor of Liverpool Prison; he later served as governor of such prisons as Dartmoor and Wormwood Scrubs, and acted as secretary to the Prison Commission. In 1913, he became head of C.I.D., which acted as the enforcement arm of British military intelligence after war broke out. When the Dutch exotic dancer and alleged spy Mata Hari arrived in England in 1916, she was arrested and interviewed at length by Thomson at Scotland Yard; she was released, only to be shot the following year by a French firing squad. He gave an account of the interrogation in *Queer People* (1922).

Thomson was knighted, and given the additional responsibility of acting as Director of Intelligence at the Home Office, but in 1921, he was controversially ousted, prompting a heated debate in Parliament: according to *The Times*, "for a few minutes there was pandemonium". The government argued that Thomson was at odds with the Commissioner of the Metropolitan Police, Sir William Horwood (whose own career ended with an ignominious departure fromoffice seven years later), but it seems likely be that covert political machinations lay behind his removal. With many aspects of Thomson's complex life, it is hard to disentangle fiction from fact.

Undaunted, Thomson resumed his writing career, and in 1925, he published *Mr Pepper Investigates*, a collection of humorous short mysteries, the most renowned of which is "The Vanishing of Mrs Fraser". In the same year, he was arrested in Hyde Park for "committing an act in violation of public decency" with a young woman who gave her name as Thelma de Lava. Thomson protested his innocence, but in vain: his trial took place amid a blaze of publicity, and he was fined five pounds. Despite the fact that Thelma de Lava had pleaded guilty (her fine was reportedly paid by a photographer), Thomson launched an appeal, claiming that he was the victim of a conspiracy, but the court would have none of it. Was he framed, or the victim of entrapment? If so, was the reason connected with his past work in intelligence or crime solving? The answers remain uncertain, but Thomson's equivocal responses to the police after being apprehended damaged his credibility.

Public humiliation of this kind would have broken a less formidable man, but Thomson, by now in his mid-sixties, proved astonishingly resilient. A couple of years after his trial, he was appointed to reorganise the Siamese police force, and he continued to produce novels. These included *The Kidnapper* (1933), which Dorothy L. Sayers described in a review for the *Sunday Times* as "not so much a detective story as a sprightly fantasia upon a detective theme." She approved the fact that Thomson wrote "good English very amusingly", and noted that "some of his characters have real charm." Mr Pepper returned in *The Kidnapper*, but in the same year, Thomson introduced his most important character, a Scottish policeman called Richardson.

Thomson took advantage of his inside knowledge to portray a young detective climbing through the ranks at Scotland Yard. And Richardson's rise is amazingly rapid: thanks to the fastest fast-tracking imaginable, he starts out as a police constable, and has become Chief Constable by the time of his seventh appearance – in a book published only four years after the first. We learn little about Richardson's background beyond the fact that he comes of Scottish farming stock, but he is likeable as well as highly efficient, and his sixth case introduces him to his future wife. His inquiries take him – and other colleagues – not only to different parts of England but also across the Channel on more than one occasion: in *The Case of the Dead Diplomat*, all the action takes place in France. There is a zest about the stories, especially when compared with some of the crime novels being produced at around the same time, which is striking, especially given that all of them were written by a man in his seventies.

From the start of the series, Thomson takes care to show the team work necessitated by a criminal investigation. Richardson is a key connecting figure, but the importance of his colleagues' efforts is never minimised in order to highlight his brilliance. In *The Case of the Dead Diplomat*, for instance, it is the trusty

Sergeant Cooper who makes good use of his linguistic skills and flair for impersonation to trap the villains of the piece. Inspector Vincent takes centre stage in *The Milliner's Hat Mystery*, with Richardson confined to the background. He is more prominent in *A Murder is Arranged*, but it is Inspector Dallas who does most of the leg-work.

Such a focus on police team-working is very familiar to present day crime fiction fans, but it was something fresh in the Thirties. Yet Thomson was not the first man with personal experience of police life to write crime fiction: Frank Froest, a legendary detective, made a considerable splash with his first novel, *The Grell Mystery*, published in 1913. Froest, though, was a career cop, schooled in "the university of life" without the benefit of higher education, who sought literary input from a journalist, George Dilnot, whereas Basil Thomson was a fluent and experienced writer whose light, brisk style is ideally suited to detective fiction, with its emphasis on entertainment. Like so many other detective novelists, his interest in "true crime" is occasionally apparent in his fiction, but although *Who Killed Stella Pomeroy?* opens with a murder scenario faintly reminiscent of the legendary Wallace case of 1930, the storyline soon veers off in a quite different direction.

Even before Richardson arrived on the scene, two accomplished detective novelists had created successful police series. Freeman Wills Crofts devised elaborate crimes (often involving ingenious alibis) for Inspector French to solve, and his books highlight the patience and meticulous work of the skilled police investigator. Henry Wade wrote increasingly ambitious novels, often featuring the Oxford-educated Inspector Poole, and exploring the tensions between police colleagues as well as their shared values. Thomson's mysteries are less convoluted than Crofts', and less sophisticated than Wade's, but they make pleasant reading. This is, at least in part, thanks to little touches of detail that are unquestionably authentic – such as senior officers' dread of newspaper criticism, as in *The Dartmoor Enigma*. No other crime writer, after all, has ever had such wide-ranging personal experience of prison management, intelligence work, the hierarchies of Scotland Yard, let alone a desperate personal fight, under the unforgiving glare of the media spotlight, to prove his innocence of a criminal charge sure to stain, if not destroy, his reputation.

Ingenuity was the hallmark of many of the finest detective novels written during "the Golden Age of murder" between the wars, and intricacy of plotting – at least judged by the standards of Agatha Christie, Anthony Berkeley, and John Dickson Carr – was not Thomson's true speciality. That said, *The Milliner's Hat Mystery* is remarkable for having inspired Ian Fleming, while he was working in intelligence during the Second World War, after Thomson's death. In a memo to Rear Admiral John Godfrey, Fleming said: "The following suggestion is used in a book by Basil Thomson: a corpse dressed as an airman, with despatches in his pockets, could be dropped on the coast, supposedly from a parachute that has failed. I understand there is no difficulty in obtaining corpses at the Naval Hospital, but, of course, it would have to be a fresh one." This clever idea became the basis for "Operation Mincemeat", a plan to conceal the invasion of Italy from North Africa.

A further intriguing connection between Thomson and Fleming is that Thomson inscribed copies of at least two of the Richardson books to Kathleen Pettigrew, who was personal assistant to the Director of MI6, Stewart Menzies. She is widely regarded as the woman on whom Fleming based Miss Moneypenny, secretary to James Bond's boss M – the Moneypenny character was originally called "Petty" Petteval. Possibly it was through her that Fleming came across Thomson's book.

Thomson's writing was of sufficiently high calibre to prompt Dorothy L. Sayers to heap praise on Richardson's performance in his third case: "he puts in some of that excellent, sober, straightforward detective work which he so well knows how to do and follows the clue of a post-mark to the heart of a very plausible and proper mystery. I find him a most agreeable companion." The acerbic American critics Jacques Barzun and Wendell Hertig Taylor also had a soft spot for Richardson, saying in *A Catalogue of Crime* that his investigations amount to "early police routine minus the contrived bickering, stomach ulcers, and pub-crawling with which later writers have masked poverty of invention and the dullness of repetitive questioning".

Books in the Richardson series have been out of print and hard to find for decades, and their reappearance at affordable prices is as welcome as it is overdue. Now that Dean Street Press have republished all eight recorded entries in the Richardson case-book, twenty-first century readers are likely to find his company just as agreeable as Sayers did.

Martin Edwards

www.martinedwardsbooks.com

Chapter One

A BIG Sunbeam touring car was crawling along the concrete road of one of the new building estates bordering on Ealing. Its occupants were gazing at the fronts of the houses on either side of the road.

"I must explain that Christine is still under the spell of this new craze for modern houses, replete with all the gadgets which become your own property as soon as you have paid the first instalment to the building society," said Herbert Mitchell to his friend Jim Milsom, who had undertaken to cart them round in his car on their house-hunting expedition.

They were friends of long standing. The Mitchells, who had been living in France from motives of economy, had lately been driven out by the persistent adherence of the French to the gold standard and the consequent high cost of living as compared with the cost in England.

"I'm not under the spell of these long rows of houses all exactly alike," protested Christine. "I was thinking of a detached bungalow somewhere—"

"Oh, but think of the pleasure you would take in your neighbours if you lived in one of these. Think of the family washing gaily flapping from the clotheslines in the back gardens on either side of you. Think of five o'clock, when the fathers come home and turn on their wireless, all playing different tunes, and then, when the green timber begins to warp, and doors and windows stick fast, you have only to bang on the party wall to bring a hefty neighbour to your rescue."

Mrs Mitchell laid a restraining hand on her driver's arm and pointed to a low building on their left. "There! Mr Milsom, that's the kind of bungalow I've been dreaming of."

"But it has already been sold and occupied," objected her husband.

"I know it has, but the architect is certain to have repeated his masterpiece somewhere else on the estate. Let's go and dig out the estate agent and take him by the throat—"

"I believe that we passed a little shanty labelled 'Estate Agency' in the last street but one," said Milsom. "I've plenty of room for turning the car. Shout when you see the notice board."

The estate agent proved to be not a man, but a very forthcoming young woman. To her Mitchell explained what they were looking for. "I'm afraid," said the young woman, "that you are too late. Eastwood was let six months ago, and the tenants are so pleased with it that they would never give it up."

"Haven't you another detached bungalow built on the same plan?" asked Christine Mitchell.

"As a matter of fact I have. It is let at present, but when I last saw Mr Miles Pomeroy, the tenant, he told me that he might be going abroad and if so he would ask me to find him another tenant to take the lease off his hands. I'll ring him up and ask him whether you could go round and see it."

She plied the telephone without success and looked at the clock. "I expect Mr Pomeroy has gone off to business, but Mrs Pomeroy ought to be there."

"Couldn't we go round in the car and see it?"

The agent looked at her engagement book. "It's early. I'll lock up the office and take you round. No doubt Mrs Pomeroy will let us go over the house; if not I'm afraid that there'll be nothing doing, unless I can tempt you with one of our other houses."

"My wife seems to have set her heart on that bungalow, Eastwood," said Mitchell. "If we can't have that or its twin sister I'm afraid that we must look elsewhere." The agent took the seat beside Jim Milsom and guided him through a network of turnings until at last they reached a bungalow even more seductive to Mrs Mitchell than Eastwood itself. It stood quite detached from its neighbours.

"Of course it won't always be so isolated," said the agent. "According to the plan other houses are to be built at a little distance, but that need not worry you: it may be months before the company begins to build, and in the meantime you have a garden front and back, a garage and a lawn nearly big enough for a tennis court. Ah, we are in luck. There is Mr Pomeroy weeding his lawn. If you'll let me out of the car I'll go and ask him whether he would like to let."

In three or four minutes she was back, followed by Pomeroy with his weeding spud in his hand. He was a man of between thirty and forty, with thinning hair and a studious look. His voice was pleasant.

"Miss Lane tells me that you would like to look over the bungalow with a view to taking it if I decide to let. I'm sure that my wife will be delighted to show you over it. She got up rather late this morning, and she may still be in the bathroom, but if you will wait for a few moments in the lounge I'll see how the land lies." He led the way into the lounge.

When they were left to themselves Mrs Mitchell looked round her. "I think that his lounge is perfect," she said. "I do hope that the lady will forgive us for calling at such an early hour—"

Her words were cut short by an almost animal roar from the back regions followed by a cry of, "Miss Lane, come quick!"

"What can have happened?" exclaimed Christine Mitchell, trembling. "Herbert, go and see whether they want help."

But Jim Milsom was before him. He halted at the bathroom door, from which the voices proceeded. He heard Miss Lane's voice; she seemed to be a competent person in an emergency. "Pull up the waste and let the water out."

"She's dead," groaned the man.

"Can I help?" called Milsom. They did not appear to have heard him. Pomeroy's voice went on:

"She must have fallen and struck her head against the taps. Look, there's blood everywhere."

"Never mind about that now. What you have to do is to telephone to your doctor to come at once."

Pomeroy passed Jim Milsom in the passage without speaking; he went straight to the telephone in the lounge and dialled a number. "Is that Dr Green? This is Miles Pomeroy speaking. I want you to come round to the bungalow at once... Yes, it's very urgent...My wife's had an accident—she's fallen in her bath and hurt herself...You can? Thank you."

He became suddenly aware of the Mitchells. "I'm sorry that you've come at such a moment. There's been an accident in the bathroom: my wife has been hurt."

"Can't I help?" asked Christine.

"No thank you. Miss Lane is doing all she can. We can do nothing until the doctor comes."

He left them and returned to the bathroom. Jim Milsom came into the lounge with Miss Lane.

"I can do nothing for her," said the agent. "She's quite dead, poor dear! We can only wait until the doctor comes."

"Well, aren't we rather in the way?" said Mitchell. "We had better go."

"No," said Milsom. "We can't leave Miss Lane to walk back to her office."

"It is very kind of you. I should be glad to have a lift back as soon as we know what the doctor says. I don't think we shall be in the way. If you stay here I'll go back to Mr Pomeroy."

"I'll tell you one thing," said Milsom in a low voice when he was alone with the Mitchells: "I looked into that bathroom. It's a shambles—blood all over the bath. That couldn't have come from banging her head on the tap."

"Nonsense, my dear fellow," said Mitchell. "That comes of all the thriller trash you have to read as a publisher; things don't happen like that in real life."

"Yes, but slipping in the bath and banging your head on the tap would make no more than a big bruise."

Christine shuddered. "Well, I don't want this bungalow now."

A motor horn sounded at the gate; a car swished up the short gravel drive. From the window they saw Dr Green—a man nearing forty, with a keen face and an air of decision. Pomeroy had heard the car and came hurrying through the lounge to meet him.

"I'm so glad you've come, Doctor," he said. "I'll take you straight to the bathroom."

In a very few moments Miss Lane returned to the lounge. "I'm afraid I may be kept for some minutes," she said. "Dr Green has asked me to telephone for Dr Leach, the police surgeon."

Milsom cocked his eye at the Mitchells. "Don't hurry, Miss Lane," he said. "We can wait."

The agent got through and sent the message. She came over to the Mitchells. "I'm so sorry that this has happened," she said.

"But you couldn't help it."

"I would have suggested your leaving me here, but Dr Green wouldn't listen to me. He says that in all these mysterious cases no one ought to leave until their statements have been taken by the proper authorities."

"He does think that there is a mystery about the case then," said Milsom.

"Yes, according to him the poor woman could not have come by that dreadful injury by a fall."

Christine Mitchell knit her brow. "But who could have done it? Could it have been a burglar?"

"Of course this house is very isolated—Oh! Here comes Dr Leach. Excuse me." Miss Lane hurried to the door and admitted a rather hard-boiled-looking person of middle age.

"Well, what's wrong here?" he asked. "I thought that you people in the garden suburb prided yourselves on your freedom from crime."

"We hope there hasn't been a crime, Dr Leach. If you'll come this way I'll take you to Dr Green in the bathroom. He'll tell you how we found the body of Mrs Pomeroy."

Having left the two doctors together she returned to the lounge with Miles Pomeroy. "The doctors sent us away; they said that in that tiny bathroom there wasn't room for us if they were to do their work, but Dr Leach was careful to say that no one must leave the house for the present."

"That won't prevent me from going to the car for my cigarette case," said Milsom, rising and going to the door. But he did not go to the car, for beside the steps he caught sight of the stub of a cigar. He picked it up and stowed it in an envelope. Then he made a perambulation of the house and garden, looking for any unusual feature, especially for scratches or heel marks on the stone window sills, for, he argued, no burglar could have got into such a house without leaving a mark. He smiled as he thought of the long face that his friend, Superintendent Richardson, would pull if he knew that he was treading on the ground that should have been sacred to the Criminal Investigation Department.

At that moment a taxi drew up as near to the gate as the other cars allowed. A young man alighted. Milsom went to meet him.

"Are you Mr Miles Pomeroy?" enquired the new arrival with a slightly patronizing air. There was a hint of a colonial accent in his speech.

"No, I'm not. Mr Pomeroy is in great trouble at this moment. Is your business with him pressing?"

"Well, as a matter of fact my business concerns Mrs Pomeroy, who is a sort of cousin of mine."

"Then I'm afraid I've bad news for you. Mrs Pomeroy met with a fatal accident this morning."

"Good God! Do you mean she's dead?"

"I'm afraid so. The doctors are with her now."

"What an extraordinary coincidence. I've come all the way from New Zealand to break the news of a death, and now I find that she herself is dead." He took out his handkerchief and wiped his brow. "This has been a bit of a shock to me."

"Well, I suppose you'd better come in and see Pomeroy." Milsom led the way into the house. "That is Mr Pomeroy," he said, pointing him out.

"I daresay you've heard of me. I'm Ted Maddox, Mr Colter's adopted son. I came to tell your wife about her uncle's death, but I've come at a bad moment. I'm sorry. Would you like me to go and come back to see you this evening?"

"Just as you like," said Pomeroy in a dull voice.

The young man seemed quite ready to make his escape. Jim Milsom saw him to the gate.

"Where are you staying?" he asked.

"I haven't an address yet. I only landed this morning and came straight on here." He produced a bulky envelope from his pocket and displayed the address, "Messrs Jackson, Burke & Company, Solicitors, Southampton Street, London, W.C."

"This contains Mr Colter's will. I was charged to bring it over, but I thought it better to see Mrs Pomeroy first. I'll go on to Southampton Street now."

When Milsom got back to the lounge the two doctors came in.

"I understand from Miss Lane," said Dr Leach, "that you were merely visiting the house as likely tenants when the body was found and that you would like to get away."

Dr Green was at the telephone, and Milsom, who was nearest to him, caught the words, "Is that the C.I.D. office? Dr Green speaking."

"Now you two gentlemen," said Dr Leach, pulling out a sheet of official foolscap from his attaché case—"I should like you each to give your name and full address on this paper and a short statement of what brought you here."

When they had finished, it came to Miss Lane's turn, and her statement had perforce to be far more detailed since she was the second person to see the body. Dr Leach read her statement through and asked, "How long would it take you to get here from your office, if the police want to question you?"

"By car, less than five minutes; on foot, of course, longer."

"Very well, then, you may go, all four of you. We can send for you if you're wanted."

As the four were taking their seats in Milsom's car another car drove up and deposited the divisional detective inspector at the gate. He had brought with him a detective sergeant.

"Back to your office I suppose, Miss Lane?" asked Milsom, sitting at the wheel.

"Yes, please. I'm very sorry to have brought you all into this tragic business, but—"

"How could you have known what we were going to find?" asked Milsom. "As long as these local police people don't keep hunting us to give evidence, I don't mind. What sort of man is Pomeroy?"

"Oh, his family is well known here. They live in Ealing—most respectable people."

"And his wife—the dead woman?"

"Oh, I never listen to gossip. If I did..."

Milsom understood. "If you did you could tell us a lot, I've no doubt. The extraordinary thing to me is to think that the husband could be quietly grubbing up weeds in his garden while his wife was being murdered in the house behind him."

"Surely she must have screamed," said Christine.

"Or she must have known the murderer," said Milsom.

"One thing I feel sure of," said Miss Lane: "it was not Mr Pomeroy; he would never have done such a thing."

"Or, if he had, he wouldn't have invited us into the house to find the body," observed Milsom. "The type of man that I take him to be could never have acted so cool a part. He would have been straining every nerve to do a bunk."

Having deposited Miss Lane at her office, Milsom turned to Christine. "Any more bungalows this morning?"

"No thank you, Mr Milsom. I've seen enough bungalows to last me a lifetime."

Chapter Two

THE TWO police officers were received at the door by Dr Leach.

"We've got a job for you, Mr Aitkin," he said to the divisional detective inspector, "and I fancy that it's going to take you all your time."

"A case of murder, Doctor?"

"Yes, it's a murder all right, but you'd better come through and see for yourself."

The two disappeared into the bathroom, leaving Dr Green and Pomeroy in the lounge. After making a cursory examination of the bathroom and scribbling a number of notes, the inspector gave the order to remove the body into the bedroom. There they laid it on the bed and covered it with a sheet.

"Get to work in the bathroom and look for fingerprints or other identification marks left by the murderer," said Inspector

Aitkin to his sergeant. Then he turned to Dr Leach. "Who was the first person to find the body?" he asked.

"Why, the husband. He found it and called to the agent, Miss Lane. I don't think that the other three people saw the body at all."

"What other three people?"

"Here are their statements with their names and addresses."

Aitkin read the statements carefully. "H'm," he grunted. "It may not be a very complicated case after all. I'll take charge of these statements. We may have to get these people down for the inquest. You're quite satisfied, Doctor, that that wound on the head could not have been caused by a fall on the taps?"

"Quite."

"There's one thing which I daresay you noticed—that pair of slippers half kicked under the bath were of men's size."

"Yes, I noticed that, too, and they were sprinkled with blood."

"Well, Sergeant Hammett is going over the bloodstains in the bathroom. Is it possible that the body was put into the bath after the blow was struck in order to make it appear that it was an accident?"

"A blow like that would have caused a lot of bleeding. Before I could accept that theory you'd have to show me another room with a trail of blood."

"It won't take us two minutes to go through all the rooms. Come along."

There were only two other bedrooms, a small sitting room and the kitchen, and all of these were entirely clear of bloodstains.

"Well then, you can concentrate your attention on the bathroom. You'll have nothing else to distract you," said Dr Leach.

Sergeant Hammett emerged from the bathroom as they approached. "This bathroom is crawling with fingerprints, Inspector. I haven't tested the walls for hidden prints, but there are quite a dozen prints made with bloody fingers. Everything points to there having been a struggle in this room: the bath mat, a brush and those slippers have all been kicked under the bath."

"You've found nothing with which the blow could have been struck?"

"Nothing, and I looked everywhere."

"You'd better have a good look round the garden outside. Now, Doctor, I shall have to take a statement from the husband. I suppose we can take it in the lounge."

"Yes, you'll find him there with Dr Green."

The inspector pulled out from his attaché case some sheets of official stationery.

"I must take a statement from you, Mr Pomeroy. Please sit down there and reply to my questions. Your name is Miles Pomeroy, I think. And you are by profession...?"

"A clerk in the Union Bank."

"Your age?"

"Thirty-six."

"How old was your wife?"

"Thirty-two."

Now, Mr Pomeroy, will you give me an account of what happened this morning. When did you last see your wife alive?"

"At half-past eight this morning."

"Did you breakfast together at that hour?"

"No, I breakfasted alone at eight. I had taken her a cup of tea at half-past seven."

"You say you last saw her at half-past eight?"

"Yes, she called to me and asked me to go to the town and buy her a grapefruit as she had no appetite for breakfast. I went, and I called in also at the newspaper shop for the *Daily Mail*. Then I came back, put the grapefruit in the dining room and called to my wife to say it was there."

"Did she answer you?"

"No, but I assumed that she was in the bathroom, and I went out to do some weeding in the garden, where Miss Lane found me."

"Where do you keep your slippers?"

"Ah! You found them in the bathroom, I suppose. The fact is that my wife was in the habit of using them in preference to her own."

"Now, Mr Pomeroy, I must give you the usual caution: that anything you say may afterwards be used in evidence. What terms were you on with your wife?"

"Oh, the usual terms of husband and wife."

"Affectionate terms?"

"Yes."

"Why are you at home today? Is your bank closed?"

"No, but I wasn't feeling very well this morning, and I telephoned to ask for a day's sick leave."

"What were you doing yesterday evening?"

"We attended a bridge party together."

"Where?"

"At the house of some friends of ours, the Claremonts."

"At what time did you get home?"

"Oh, it was a little past midnight. We walked home."

"You had no quarrel?"

"Oh dear no. We don't quarrel over games."

"Do you occupy the same bedroom?"

"No, neither of us sleep very well, and for some months we have used separate rooms."

"Well, Mr Pomeroy, I must ask you to stay here at the disposal of the coroner. You must on no account leave the neighbourhood."

"Certainly, but I suppose I can go to the bank daily as usual?"

"Yes."

Dr Green came forward. "If you don't want me any longer, I feel that I ought to be seeing my patients."

"Certainly, Doctor. We'll let you know when you're wanted for the inquest. I'd like a word with you, Dr Leach," the inspector said to the police surgeon in a lower voice.

Pomeroy took the hint and showed Dr Green to the door.

"Everything points rather strongly to the husband," said the inspector, "but I can't very well detain him without charging him, and I shall have to consult higher authority before doing that." As Pomeroy rejoined them he said, "You must have noticed, Mr Pomeroy, that there were a number of fingerprints on the wall of the bathroom. Would you have any objection to going through the formality of allowing me to take your fingerprints?"

"I fancy that the prints you noticed in the bathroom must all be mine. I had to put my hands on the wall when I was lifting my wife's body; but by all means take my fingerprints if you have the materials here."

Inspector Aitkin motioned to his sergeant, who took from his attaché case a slip of zinc, a bottle of printing ink, and a tiny roller of rubber with which to spread the ink evenly over the zinc.

"Now sir," said Inspector Aitkin, "leave your muscles quite loose; it won't take a minute." Bringing the inked plate to the edge of the table and laying beside it a folded sheet of paper, Aitkin rolled each of Pomeroy's fingertips on the plate and transferred the ink to the appropriate space on the paper. Having completed the right hand, he poured a few drops of benzine on a cloth and wiped off the ink. "Now sir, your left hand." The operation was repeated. Aitkin had now a complete record of the rolled prints; there remained only to take a simultaneous print of the four fingers of each hand. This having been completed, Sergeant Hammett stowed away the apparatus in his attaché case while his inspector led the way to the bathroom. He pulled out a magnifying lens and compared the imprints on the wall with the prints he had just taken.

"Yes, Mr Pomeroy, you were right. These impressions were left by your fingers."

"If you don't want me any more just now, I'd like to go and tell my mother what's happened."

"Certainly, but you understand that you must not go anywhere without telling us where you can be found? "Yes, I quite understand that."

"I must be off too, Inspector, if you can spare me," said Dr Leach. "You and Hammett have work to do, I expect."

Left to himself, Aitkin returned to the bathroom and was busy applying his reading glass to the marks on the walls when Sergeant Hammett appeared at the door.

"I've just found this in that little ornamental pond behind the house," he said; "I got it out with the garden rake." He held up a coal hammer still wet from immersion.

"Be careful how you handle it," said Aitkin; "those brown stains on it will turn out to be bloodstains unless I'm much mistaken, and the question will arise whether they were made some time before immersion and, of course, whether the blood is human. Happily that is not a matter on which we shall be called to give evidence. What we have to verify first is how the murderer, whoever he may have been, got into the house."

"The windows were all securely fastened; so was the back door: I've seen to that."

"How does the front door open?"

"Apparently only with a latchkey. The man, if he was a stranger, could only have got in by having the door opened to him by someone from inside—of course Pomeroy would have had his own latchkey. Have you made up your mind, sir, in which room the murder was committed?"

"There's not a shadow of doubt about that. It was here in this bathroom. The woman was standing when the blow was struck: you see the blood spurted up to the ceiling." He pointed to one or two splashes on the whitewash.

"She wasn't wearing her nightdress at the time. Here it is hanging on this peg and only a few drops of blood on it, so she must have been wearing nothing but her dressing gown when the murderer came in. It seems to me that the woman was just going to step into her bath when the doorbell rang or when someone came in with a latchkey, and she slipped on her dressing gown, which is drenched with blood, as you see.

"Now the next thing to do is to verify Pomeroy's statement that he bought a grapefruit and a newspaper in the town this morning."

"There is a grapefruit on the table in the dining room."

"But we don't know whether it was bought this morning."

"No sir, but I'll find out."

"And while you're about it get hold of the milk and the bread roundsmen and ask them if they noticed any stranger about. While you're away I will go carefully round the house."

Aitkin's more minute search on the outside of the house produced nothing. The weather had been dry for some days and it was useless to search for footprints, but Aitkin did establish the fact that behind the garden lay a tract of undergrowth which ran down to the public road. This was thick enough to conceal any person approaching the bungalow from behind, or escaping from it into the public road. Clearly this undergrowth had been used for this purpose, for brambles had been trampled down or brushed aside. He had just completed a survey of this waste ground when something brown attracted his attention. A clumsy attempt seemed to have been made to conceal it by dragging or kicking the brambles into a kind of knot, but Aitkin was wearing stout boots and he found it easy to hook out the object with his toe. It was a raincoat which had seen wear. Some attempt had been made to fold it into as small a compass as possible, but it was discoloured by stains which Aitkin recognized at once as having been made by fresh blood: the stains were still red. He spread out the garment on the ground and found that it was one of those coats that are manufactured largely by machinery. One can buy them by the dozen in any clothier's, and it is the exception for any of them to bear a label indicating the shop where it was sold. All that this particular coat bore was the heraldic sign of a white horse, but coats of this brand are sold everywhere, and it would be useless to attempt to find the shop that had any record of the purchaser. Aitkin returned to the bungalow carrying the coat and hung it up on a peg in the entrance lounge to await Pomeroy's return. His sergeant was the first to appear. He reported that he had questioned the roundsmen who delivered milk and bread, and that they had seen no stranger hanging about the bungalow that morning. They said that Mr Pomeroy himself had opened the door to them.

"Did you find out where he bought the grapefruit?"

"Yes, the people at the shop knew him personally as a customer. He was there just before nine."

"And the newspaper?"

"That was not so sure. The woman at the news agent's wasn't certain that she'd seen him this morning. Did you have any luck in your search, sir?"

"Yes," said Aitkin, going to the coat pegs. "I found this. You see the blood has not had time to turn brown. It's a common kind of coat."

"Yes, in more than half the houses in this settlement you'd find a coat like that, but that's the coat the murderer must have been wearing."

"Yes, and if it belongs to Pomeroy it would be sufficient to account for the absence of bloodstains on the clothes he is wearing."

"You think that Pomeroy did it?"

"I don't see who else it could have been. At any rate we must assume that it was Pomeroy, but I doubt if Superintendent Richardson will allow us to arrest him on the evidence we have. Pomeroy mustn't be allowed to get away, or we shall hear more of it. I don't suppose he'll come back here; he will stay and have lunch with his people in Ealing. I wonder if we can find another latchkey in his desk or somewhere?"

"Better look in his dead wife's vanity bag: she is sure to have had one," said Hammett. He was, at the moment, searching a bag which he had found lying on the kitchen dresser. "Here, try this key."

"Right," called Aitkin from the door; "it fits. Now come along, and we'll call on the Pomeroy family."

"Taking the coat with us?"

"No, you can take that down to the police station, and I'll go alone to the Pomeroys and try to find out what plans Pomeroy has made. There's one thing certain: he won't want to pass another night in the bungalow after what's happened. We've plenty to do. There's the body to get down to the mortuary for the inquest; there's the coroner to be notified and the undertaker to be seen. That must be done before we go to lunch."

When Aitkin rang the bell at the house of the Pomeroy family it was clear that it was in a flutter. A rather grubby little maid came to the door.

"Missus can't see no one," she blurted out almost before Inspector Aitkin had intimated his wishes. It was the first time that this child had been mixed up in a case of murder, and she was enjoying it to the full.

Aitkin took a card from his pocket and said, "It is not Mrs Pomeroy that I have come to see, but her son."

"You can't see him neither. No, you can't see him whoever you are." She was for slamming the door in his face, but he put a foot against it and assumed an air of severity.

"Take that card to Mr Miles Pomeroy and tell him that I must see him at once."

"You can't see anyone in this house," returned the damsel stoutly. "Them's my orders."

"Then I must give you fresh orders, young woman. Take that card in to Mr Miles Pomeroy and say that I'm waiting to see him in the hall."

Very unwillingly the young woman retired to a sitting room on the ground floor, from which Miles Pomeroy emerged.

"I've called to ask you one question, Mr Pomeroy. Do you possess a fawn-coloured raincoat?"

"No. I had one until some days ago, and then my wife took it to send to some connection of hers in another part of the country."

"Do you remember what label it had on the inside of the collar?"

"I don't think it had any label; I don't remember noticing one."

"Do you know the address of the person your wife sent it to?"

"No, I'm sorry, I don't. It was someone who wrote to her for help."

"I see. Thank you. That is all I want to ask just now."

Inspector Aitkin left the house with a confident smile upon his features.

Chapter Three

Two DAYS after their adventure on the Ealing estate Jim Milsom rang up his friend Herbert Mitchell.

"Is that you, Herbert? Milsom speaking. You're coming down to the inquest, of course?"

"No, they haven't subpoenaed me."

"What does that matter? They've left me out too, but we have a duty to perform. We've got to see that Pomeroy has a fair 'do.' I'll come round with the car and drive you down. It's a public enquiry, and we'll jolly well see that justice is done."

On the way down they discussed the case. "You'll see," said Milsom, "that the police have got together every scrap of evidence that bears against Pomeroy and haven't worried themselves about any other possible malefactor."

"Well, that's quite natural, isn't it? Who else could it be but Pomeroy? Oh, I know what you'll say—that Pomeroy isn't at all the kind of person to commit a murder—but remember that still waters run deep and these innocent-looking culprits are very often born actors."

"I hope to goodness the coroner is a discriminating bloke. He may have something up his sleeve that we know nothing about."

The two took their seats unobtrusively in the coroner's court—a bare room which was used for dances and concerts and was furnished with the hardest kind of chair that people can be condemned to sit upon. The jury had already been sworn, and the coroner, a man who knew his job, had been furnished by the police with the results of enquiries that had been made about the bridge party at the house of the Claremonts on the evening before the murder. It was of a sensational character. Though it had no direct bearing upon the crime, the coroner determined to bring it before the jury through the witnesses who had been present. In his opening charge to the jury he explained that even trivial incidents might have a bearing upon their verdict. First he called Miss Lane, who described her meeting with Mr Pomeroy on the morning of the murder. She said that he was quietly weeding the lawn in his garden; that he seemed quite normal and in no way disturbed in manner; that he led the way into the lounge and went to the bathroom to see whether his wife was in a fit state to receive them. Then she described his cry for help and what she found in the bathroom. No questions were put to her.

"Edward Green," called the coroner. Dr Green took his place at the witness stand. After the usual questions about his qualifications, the coroner asked him, "Were you the regular medical attendant of the deceased woman?"

"I was."

"Would you describe her as a person of normal health?"

"Yes, physically she was, but she had fits of cerebral excitement when perhaps she would not act normally."

"In simpler language you would say that she had a bad temper?"

"Yes, and when in that condition she would not have full command of her language or her acts."

"On the morning of September thirteenth were you called to her by telephone?"

"I was. Mr Pomeroy took me into the bathroom, where I found the deceased lying against the end of the bath. I sent Miss Lane to telephone to Dr Leach."

"In what state was the body?"

"The woman seemed to have been dead for a little over an hour; the body had not begun to stiffen. When I reached the bathroom the water had been run off and the bath was empty. The shoulders were lying against the taps, but the head had fallen forward on the chest. There was a deep scalp wound on the top of the head which had produced a fracture of the skull. That, undoubtedly, was the cause of death."

"Was it the sort of blow that might have been made by this hammer?" asked the coroner, holding up a hammer. Dr Green took the tool in his hand and weighed it.

"Yes sir, it may have been an implement like this."

There was corroborative evidence from Dr Leach. The coroner now called Divisional Detective Inspector Aitkin, who deposed to having made a detailed inspection of the bathroom and other parts of the little house.

"Did you find evidence of there having been a struggle in the bathroom?" asked the coroner.

"Yes sir, there had been some kind of struggle just inside the door. The bath sponge, the brush and the bath mat had been kicked or pushed under the bath. It looked to me as if the woman had been standing when she received the blow, for blood had spurted up to the ceiling."

"You found fingerprints?"

"Yes sir, some of them stained with blood."

"Whose were they?"

"Those of Miles Pomeroy, the husband. I have brought his prints here for the jury to compare with photographs of the prints on the bathroom wall."

"Did you find any other prints in the bathroom?"

"No sir."

"There were men's bedroom slippers near the bath?"

"Yes sir, but Mr Pomeroy explained that his wife was in the habit of using his slippers when she went to her bath."

"Did you find any bloodstained clothes about the house or in the bathroom?"

"Yes sir, the deceased's nightdress with only a splash or two was hanging on a hook behind the door, but her dressing gown drenched with blood was lying in a heap on the floor."

"You found none of Mr Pomeroy's clothes stained with blood?"

"No sir."

"Neither on the clothes he was wearing nor on any of his clothing in the house?"

"Only on the left sleeve of the coat he was wearing, which could have got there when he lifted the body."

"Did you notice any indications of there having been a robbery in the house?"

"No sir."

"Or any sign of breaking in?"

"No sir."

"This hammer—where did you find it?"

"Sergeant Hammett found it at the bottom of the little ornamental pond. He got it out with a garden rake."

"Did you enquire whether any strangers had been seen near the house that morning?"

"I did, sir, but without result."

"I understand that the bungalow is rather isolated from the other houses on the estate."

"Yes sir, it stands quite alone and out of sight of the other houses."

"Where was this coat found?" The coroner held up the bloodstained raincoat.

"I found it rolled up in the undergrowth behind the bungalow which runs down to the public road."

"Had Miles Pomeroy a raincoat like this?"

"No sir. Mr Miles Pomeroy stated that he had had a coat like this, but that his wife had given it away about a fortnight ago."

The coroner now called Jane Trefusis, a vivacious-looking woman in the early thirties.

"You were one of the guests at a bridge party on the evening before Mrs Pomeroy met her death?"

"I was."

"And you were playing at the same table?"

"Yes, we four ladies were playing at one table; we had drawn for partners, and it happened that way. The four men played at a separate table."

"The deceased woman, Mrs Pomeroy, was your partner?"

"No, she was playing with Mrs Meadows."

"Did anything unusual happen during the game?"

"Yes. Mrs Meadows was losing. She said laughingly, 'It's this opal-and-diamond ring I'm wearing. I'll take it off while I deal.' She was in the middle of dealing when the electric light failed. When it came on again the ring had disappeared. Nobody had been near the table in the darkness except we four ladies. Our exclamations brought Mr Meadows over from the other table. He was much upset. 'There's only one thing to do,' he said: 'we must turn out the lights and see whether the ring comes back.' As nobody objected at the time, this was done. Nobody moved while the lights were out, and then, when they were switched on again, the ring was there. Then we all objected very strongly, since it left three of us under suspicion. Mrs Pomeroy lost her temper and accused Mrs Meadows of having hidden the ring as a practical joke. Her husband tried to calm her, but that only made her worse.

He apologized to the rest of us and took her home. "We could hear her angry recrimination even when the front door had been shut."

The next witness called was Police Sergeant Steggles.

"You are station sergeant at Ealing?"

"Yes sir."

"Do you remember a charge being brought against the deceased woman, Stella Pomeroy?"

"Yes sir, a charge of shoplifting two years ago, but she was acquitted."

"What was the attitude of her husband on that occasion?"

"He was very angry with her, and at first he refused to go home with her; afterwards he calmed down, and they went away together."

The next witness was Margaret Close, who said that she was a charwoman employed by several householders. She was engaged by Mrs Pomeroy for two hours three times a week.

"Were you ever present when there were quarrels between Mr Pomeroy and his wife?"

"Was I not, sir! They was at it all the time, about one thing or another. I tell you that I was sorry for the poor man what he had to put up with. I didn't wonder when he lost his temper as he did sometimes."

"Call Miles Pomeroy," said the coroner.

The court rustled with anticipation as Pomeroy walked to the witness stand. After giving an account of his movements on the fatal morning, he was questioned by the coroner about the incidents at the bridge party. He confirmed the account given by Mrs Trefusis.

"When the ring disappeared from the ladies' bridge table had you any suspicion against any of them?"

"No."

"I put it to you that after that charge of shoplifting of which your wife was acquitted, you did accuse her of having abstracted the ring when the lights were out and of having put it back when the lights were extinguished for the second time."

The witness hesitated.

"Surely you can remember what you said to your wife on the way home."

"I may have said something like that."

"And she, very naturally, resented it."

"Yes, but I said nothing more. I shut myself into my room."

"Did you continue your quarrel in the morning?"

"No. I got up early and made her a cup of tea and took it to her room."

"How did she receive you?"

"Oh, quite in a friendly way. She seemed grateful. She told me she was not feeling very well and that she would not get up very early."

"You had said something to the agent, Miss Lane, a week or two ago, about letting your bungalow, but you had not definitely put it into her hands."

"That is so."

"And yet your wife was surprised to hear from Miss Lane a few days afterwards that you thought of leaving."

"I had not discussed it with her."

"Why was that? Surely she had as great an interest as you had."

"The question was still in embryo. It depended upon my getting a transfer to one of our foreign branches."

"Had you applied for such a transfer?"

"Yes."

"Without telling your wife?"

"Yes."

"Can you explain this to the jury?"

"If I had succeeded in getting a job abroad I intended to propose to my wife that we should separate on terms as favourable as I could make them."

"Will you look at this hammer," said the coroner, "and tell the jury whether you recognize it as belonging to you."

"It looks very like the hammer we used for breaking coal, but I can't swear to it. It's a very common type of hammer."

"Take it in your hand and look at the handle. It has a P scratched on it, and that is your initial."

"Then it must be mine."

"Had your wife any enemy who might wish to injure her?"

"Not that I know of. I think she would have told me if she had."

"How long were you absent from the house that morning?"

"I left about half-past eight, did my shopping and was back about half-past nine."

"Did you notice whether the house looked normal when you came back?"

"Yes, quite normal. I did not go to my wife's room because I was afraid that I might wake her. I went out and did some weeding."

"You did not go to the bank that day?"

"No sir, I telephoned to the bank to say that I was not feeling well enough to come."

"And yet you were well enough to weed your garden."

"Yes, and I should have been well enough to go to the bank, but I intended to thrash out the whole question of our separation with my wife that morning as soon as she was dressed."

The coroner held up the bloodstained coat found by Inspector Aitkin and asked, "Did this coat belong to you? Take it in your hand and look at the trademark under the collar."

The witness examined the coat and said with emphasis, "No, that is not mine."

"You had one like it."

"Yes, but my wife gave it away about a fortnight ago."

"To whom?"

"She never told me."

"But surely she would mention a thing like that to you."

"No, not necessarily. She had a number of actor friends who used to write her begging letters, and then she would look through my wardrobe and send some worn-out garment and forget about it until I began to hunt for it."

"Have you the address of any of these people?"

"No, I never troubled to ask her who they were."

The coroner told him to stand down and began his address to the jury.

"In this case," he said, "you have heard witnesses proving that the deceased met a violent death at the hands of some person who made a clumsy attempt to let it appear that the death had been an accident. It is not at all clear that the deceased received that blow on the head while she was in the bath. It will seem to you more likely that the murderer, whoever he was, put the body into the bath after he had killed her. You have heard the evidence of the husband; you have gathered that there were serious causes of disagreement between the couple—causes so serious that the husband had resolved upon a separation. The wife was a woman of violent temper, and you have only the husband's word for it that the quarrel of the night before was not resumed in the morning, but let me now give you a word of warning.

"Whatever verdict you give in accordance with your oaths will not affect the course of justice. You have to consider whether the evidence against the husband, or any other person, would be sufficient to convict him in a court of law. You may consider the evidence to be sufficient to convince you that no one but the husband had the opportunity for committing the crime and that no one else had a sufficient motive for committing it, but it does not follow from this that it would be wise on your part to fasten the crime upon any individual when you have the alternative of bringing in a verdict of murder against some person unknown. You have to remember that the person who committed this murder must have been deluged with the blood of his victim, and yet the police have found only one garment stained with blood, and the ownership of that garment is not yet established. If you were to return a verdict of murder against the husband he would at once forfeit his liberty and perhaps be prejudiced in his defence. This might be a very grave injustice, for you must remember that the police will continue their investigations quite independently of any verdict you may return, and therefore an open verdict such as that which I suggest to you will be a far safer course for you to adopt. Gentlemen, consider your verdict."

The jury laid their heads together and then intimated through their foreman that they would like to retire. The coroner's officer took charge of them, and they filed out.

At the back of the hall Herbert Mitchell, with his friend Jim Milsom, engaged in a whispered conversation.

"I've seen a lot of these coroner's juries," said Milsom. "Did you notice that little rat-faced blighter trying to stampede his fellow jurymen into a verdict? He's the real cantankerous little tradesman who is the curse of his nonconformist minister, and you'll see when he lets himself go in the jury room he'll worry the life out of those sober slab-sided fellow jurymen of his into bringing in a verdict against Pomeroy just because the coroner told them not to."

"Or because the evidence is pretty strong against him," said Mitchell.

"Well, you wait and see. I give him ten minutes to bring those heavy-wits round to his way of thinking."

"And if they do bring in such a verdict what's going to be done about it?"

"Well, I suppose that the coroner will have to sign a warrant committing that poor devil to prison, and it will be the devil's own job to get him out of it. There, what did I tell you—" he pointed to the clock—"the ten minutes are up and the jury are filing back into their places. Look at my rat-faced friend. He's triumphant for, you see, he feels that he's served his country by downing a paid official."

"Gentlemen, have you considered your verdict?" asked the coroner. The foreman stood up.

"Yes sir. We find that the deceased" (the worthy man pronounced the word 'diseased') "met her death at the hands of her husband, Miles Pomeroy."

"I have nothing to do but to record your verdict, but I think it right to say that in reporting your verdict to the proper authority I shall record my opinion that it is against the weight of evidence."

"What did I tell you," said Milsom. "I've attended a dozen of these inquests, but this, I think, takes the cake. It was quite obvious from the evidence that some garment worn by the murderer was smothered in blood, and it is up to the police to find out who owned that raincoat. I don't think much of that Inspector Aitkin, do you?"

"I don't think he's a flyer," said Mitchell. "He didn't seem to me to have covered the ground. Of course, when we reached the house that morning Pomeroy was perfectly at ease, and when he found his wife's body in the bathroom he was half demented."

"Exactly. I'm sure that he wasn't acting. Besides, the woman was dead when we arrived, and yet Pomeroy took us into the house. If he'd been guilty all he had to do was to say that his wife wasn't well enough to receive visitors, and then plan his escape from the murder charge. There's one man at the Yard and only one, so far as I know, who would tackle this case with success, and that's a fellow named Richardson, the youngest of the superintendents. I wonder whether, if I went round there, I could get him sent down? I know the head of the C.I.D. slightly— well enough, at any rate, to get an interview with him."

While they were talking the divisional detective inspector had come over to Pomeroy with the coroner's warrant in his hand. Beyond a strained look in Pomeroy's eyes he received the intimation that he was a prisoner quite calmly.

Chapter Four

It was characteristic of that would-be protagonist in criminology, Jim Milsom, that he should push himself to the front, dragging the more modest Mitchell with him, to volunteer his own opinion upon the bloodstained raincoat, but he was brought up against a physical as well as a moral barrier: the police seemed to ignore his presence, and they opposed a rampart of broad official backs to his approach. One cannot slap an official back in order to open diplomatic negotiations. There is nothing in life so daunting as the back of a policeman.

"We don't seem to be wanted here," observed Milsom. "If we're to do any good we shall have to take those official backs in flank."

"What do you mean?"

"That we go to Scotland Yard and beard the head of the C.I.D. They may, of course, take exception to our faces and push us politely down the granite steps into the street, but in that case we should be no worse off than we are now."

Mitchell looked at his watch. "Isn't this the sacred hour of lunch, when no self-respecting civil servant is to be found in his office?"

"That's all right, I'll take you in my car to the club. We'll lunch there comfortably and give them time to return to the pursuit of the lawless. I want to catch my friend Morden before he gets himself immersed in documents."

Jim Milsom's style of driving through the suburbs to the centre of London was a trial to his companion's nerves. He drove well and he drove boldly, yet the most pernickety of traffic officers could have found no fault with him since the needle of his speedometer never exceeded thirty in the built-up area.

"I must warn you not to expect a gargantuan feast at the Sleuths'," said Milsom. "We're a new club, run upon economical lines. But for that our membership would be small. We demand no qualification for membership; there is no detective background to the club. Any fool can call himself a Sleuth if he wants a cheap lunching place and can afford to pay the entrance fee. If he expects to hear lectures on the analysis of dust found in a coat pocket he doesn't come to us."

They were nearing the square in which the Sleuths had established themselves. It was a square of departed grandeur, dating from the regency, where members were free to park their cars under the direction of a beery-looking ex-soldier with a walrus moustache. It was he who directed Jim Milsom to his anchorage and assured him that everything he left in the car would be quite safe.

The club cook, while not enjoying a decoration from the Association of Chefs, understood how to fry sole and roast joints.

Mitchell glanced round the room, which now was fairly full. This was plainly a young man's club: scarce one of the lunchers had been born thirty years before, and none could be pronounced a student of detective science.

At half-past two Milsom consulted his wrist watch and pronounced it time to beard the head of criminal investigation in his den. In five minutes they were climbing the granite steps of the building that had been intended for an opera house in the days of Mapleson to the little centre hall where visitors are required to inscribe their names and their business on a form. The attendant constable could give them no information as to whether Mr Morden could be seen. They sat down before the window opening upon the Embankment and composed themselves to wait.

"The mills grind slowly here," said Milsom, "unless there is really startling information to impart. I suppose that if we had rushed in and announced that a mob carrying the red flag was marching upon the palace of Westminster we might have galvanized the machine into action; as it is we must sit here killing time until Charles Morden has digested his lunch."

"Probably someone else has got in before us—some time-waster who won't take No for an answer," observed Mitchell, and as if to confirm his suggestion, a messenger in plain clothes entered the hall with a ticket in his hand and looked about him. He approached the two sitting in the window.

"Mr Milsom?" he asked. "Mr Morden is sorry to have kept you waiting. If you will follow me you may see him now."

The head of the department, whose room was on the second floor adjoining that of the commissioner, received his visitors with a weary smile of welcome. He had the appearance of a man who was grossly over-worked. He rose to shake hands, and Milsom introduced his companion Mitchell.

"We haven't come to waste your time, but only to prevent if we can a serious miscarriage of justice. Probably you have not yet heard of the case, but no doubt it will come before you in due course." He described as shortly as possible the position of affairs that had led to the arrest of Miles Pomeroy on the coroner's warrant.

"I don't think that the case has come before me yet. I gather that you both disagree with the coroner's jury."

"Yes, we were present in the bungalow when Pomeroy discovered the body of his wife in the bathroom, and we were all convinced that he was not acting then. Besides, why should he have taken us, three strangers, into a house where he knew that his wife was lying dead? It would have been so easy for him to say that he was not letting the house and thus to give himself several hours in which to plan his escape."

"Or if he were a consummate actor he might have thought it a good way to prove his innocence."

"If he was acting a part, then he would have made a fortune on the stage."

"I'm afraid that impressions of that kind would weigh very little with a judge and jury. Quite a number of criminals discover unexpected histrionic talent when they find themselves 'up against it.' If you've nothing but Pomeroy's looks and demeanour to go upon I think that it would be wiser to leave the question of his guilt or innocence to the police."

"Of course you may think it presuming on our part to butt into one of your cases, but we have the excuse that we were among the first people to find the body in the bungalow, and in that way we were better qualified to judge of Pomeroy's demeanour than anyone who gave evidence at the inquest."

"You attended the inquest?" asked Morden in some surprise.

"We did, and we formed a definite opinion that Pomeroy was innocent. That is why we have come to you. Besides, the verdict of the jury was entirely against the coroner's direction."

"Well then, if they refused to listen to the coroner he is bound to have reported the case to the home secretary and some action will be taken."

Morden half rose from his seat as a hint that their conference was at an end. The two visitors took the hint. "We mustn't take up any more of your time," said Milsom, opening the door to let Mitchell pass out. Then, half closing it, he turned to Morden, saying, "I fancy that that inspector of yours at Ealing will end by landing you in a mess. Why don't you send that Superintendent Richardson down to take over the job before the local men mess it all up?"

Morden laughed. "What you would really like to ask me is, 'Why don't you turn out of that chair and let me sit in it?'"

"The country might do worse."

"The country has got on pretty well for the last few centuries with square men in round holes," observed Morden with a quiet smile, but as soon as he was alone this did not prevent him from following his practice of clearing up each case as it came along. He rang up the chief constable of the C.I.D.

"Have you had any report about a murder in one of those new building estates at Ealing, Mr Beckett—a man arrested for murder on the coroner's warrant?"

"I have a message on my table—just came in. Would you like me to come up?"

"Please do so and bring the superintendent with you."

Mr Beckett looked into the superintendent's room. "The chief wants us both upstairs, Mr Witchard."

"Why, what's up?"

"It's about that murder case down at Ealing—a man named Pomeroy. The message came through last night."

"Some busybody from outside has been getting at the chief, I suppose: that's how time gets wasted in this building."

The chief constable, a man grown grey in the service in which he had risen from the ranks by sheer merit, rose wearily from his desk and entered the lift. Morden received his two lieutenants with an amiable smile. They had brought with them two teletype messages, the only documents that had reached the Central Office thus far. Morden read the messages leisurely and asked how soon a report from the divisional detective inspector might be expected.

"It ought to have been in by now," growled Beckett. "D. D. Inspector Aitkin has no method in his work."

"He means well, but certainly he's not one of our fliers," observed Morden. "I have just received a visit from two men who claim to have been present when the woman's body was found and to have attended the inquest. Both appear to be convinced of the husband's innocence. Their object in coming to me was to try to get the case transferred to Superintendent Richardson, but Richardson is superintendent of the group of divisions in which Ealing lies, is he not?"

"Yes sir."

"Then tell him to take over the case personally and keep us informed of every step."

The instruction was not needed, for Richardson had already taken over the investigation, with Divisional Detective Inspector Aitkin working under him. His first question to Aitkin was: "Have you yourself formed any impression of the case, Mr Aitkin? Do you believe as the jury did that Pomeroy was guilty?"

"I do, Superintendent."

"On what grounds?"

"On several. First there was the quarrel at the house where they played cards on the previous evening and the evidence that for some time the two had been on bad terms."

"But a husband may be on bad terms with his wife without resorting to murder."

"Yes, but there had been this talk of separation; of Pomeroy getting a job in one of the foreign branches."

"And so you think that the husband murdered her in the bathroom and then invited strangers into the house to find the body?"

"Yes, to divert suspicion from himself by acting surprised on finding the body."

"On the other hand he may have thought that when once appointed manager of a foreign branch he would be quit of the woman without any resort to violence."

"The only fingerprints found in the bathroom were his."

"That's not surprising, since on finding the body he lifted the head out of the water, and, naturally, his hands became stained with blood. No, Inspector, I'm afraid it will take more than that to convince me."

"Well, it would have had to be quick work on the part of a stranger, and in spite of all our enquiries we have no evidence of any stranger having been in the neighbourhood."

"Well, I shall go down and have a look at the spot where that raincoat was found."

"Would you like me to come with you?"

"No, you've other work to get on with, and I would like to form my own opinion on the spot. I can easily find my way to that thicket you spoke of."

It was one of those September days which come to remind humanity of the past glories of summer without the heat. The rough turf was spangled with cobwebs glistening with dewdrops, and there was already a tang of autumn in the air.

Richardson found the hiding place of the bloodstained coat without difficulty. He was on the lookout for footprints, and there was no dearth of them. All the world seemed to have been engaged in making footprints that morning. Fortunately they were not difficult to distinguish. Those of the inspector who had discovered the coat cried out for recognition; he had been wearing substantial boots, reminiscent in their build of the boots that he had worn when in uniform. But there was a crisscross of other footprints, doubtless because this was public ground and on the first news of the tragedy every curious person in the neighbourhood had flocked to the scene. While Richardson's keen eyes were fixed upon the ground he caught the sound of rustling among the saplings of the plantation: someone was moving cautiously among the branches. If his movements were to be spied upon he must at least discover the identity of the spy; if it was to be a game of hide-and-seek he would be cast for the part of the seeker. He fell back for a few paces before plunging into the thicket at the roadside and making a rapid detour to take the spy in flank. He could move in the undergrowth as silently as a cat, and he pressed on until he became aware of a figure moving obliquely through the saplings before him. He stopped to watch, and it was some time before he could make up his mind whether the figure was that of a boy or of a young woman. Clearly the person was searching for something, and that must be his concern. He advanced boldly, taking no thought for the noise he was making, and before he quite realized it he found himself in the presence of a girl in the early twenties. She was not in the least abashed by his appearance.

"Looking for something?" he asked.

"Yes."

"What have you lost?"

"I haven't lost anything."

"Then why look for it?"

"Suppose I told you that I was a botanist looking for a rare plant."

Richardson cast an appraising eye on the brambles. "I should say that you wouldn't find it here."

"Have you lost anything?" she asked with cold politeness.

"If I were to tell you what brought me here you wouldn't believe me, and if I told you what has brought you here—namely, a morbid curiosity—you wouldn't be pleased."

"It was not morbid curiosity, and if I told you what brought me, you wouldn't believe me."

"Why beat about the bush? I'm an officer in the Criminal Investigation Department."

"Ho! Ho! Hunting for clues. Well, that's what I'm hunting for, because Miles Pomeroy is my cousin, and you clever, cunning detectives are trying to fasten a crime on an innocent man."

"Now we are really introduced, why not pool our discoveries? You may have heard my name—Superintendent Richardson of the C.I.D."

"And I'm Ann Pomeroy—a writer. You may not have heard of me, because my writings have not yet set any river on fire."

Richardson could not help feeling the antagonism which her tone intended to convey. He could not blame her after the jury's finding.

"Let me remind you that your cousin's misfortune came not from the police, but from the verdict of the coroner's jury. I, for one, am approaching the case with an entirely open mind."

She appeared a little mollified. "I can quite see that from the police point of view things look black against my cousin."

"Tell me this. Do you know him well, and did you see him often?"

"Yes, I live with his father and mother only a mile away. I saw him at least once a week. I can tell you," she added passionately, "that this is killing his mother. I'm determined to prove his innocence if the police are too stupid to do it."

"The police are not going to give the case up, if that's what you mean, and they're always glad of help from wherever it may come. You, for example, might tell me some details about your cousin and his wife."

She brought to bear on him a pair of steady grey eyes set wide apart beneath an intellectual brow.

"I feel somehow that I can trust you with family secrets. My cousin wasn't happy in his home life. Perhaps you knew that already?"

"I think that was made clear at the inquest. What I should like to know is whether Mrs Pomeroy had any special friends or enemies—"

"Friends!" She hesitated a moment. "She had one friend who was the most dangerous kind of friend that such a woman could have."

"You mean he was her lover?"

"Yes—a man who took advantage of her husband's daily absence to visit her at any hour." She paused again, then added significantly, "Even at a very early hour."

"You mean to imply...?"

"Yes," she said, "I mean to imply that Dennis Casey should now be in my cousin's place."

Chapter Five

AFTER ANOTHER twenty minutes' conversation, Richardson left Ann Pomeroy in thoughtful mood and returned to the concrete road on which stood the bungalow. He was surprised to find how little curiosity seemed to have been excited by the murder, which must be known from one end of the villa settlement to the other. He was at that moment the only pedestrian in sight, although probably he was not unobserved from behind the lace blinds in the front windows on either side of the street. The breadwinners had departed in crowded trains to the metropolis, and soon after six o'clock they would be back again with their families.

The point that was occupying Richardson's thoughts at the moment was that in all England it would be difficult to find so unlikely a stage for a murder. Even in the light of the hints given to him by Ann Pomeroy it was hard to believe in so squalid a tragedy having defaced this prim setting, and yet murder had been done and he was there to probe the mystery to the bottom. If the girl had not been unconsciously embroidering the truth he had now a good deal to go upon. The man she suspected of being Mrs Pomeroy's lover was a journalist, Dennis Casey, who, from the nature of his occupation, left for the city at an hour later than Miles Pomeroy and could easily reach the bungalow by nine every morning when Pomeroy had departed for his bank. But if this was a habit, surely it could not have escaped the notice of neighbours. True, no neighbours were living in actual sight of the bungalow, but they were passing up and down the road at all hours and must have noticed so regular a visitor. In these residential estates gossip runs on winged feet.

Where ought his enquiries to begin? Ann Pomeroy had confided to him that Casey lodged in a two-storied house at the far end of the estate, occupied by a Mrs Coxon, also Irish, with three mischievous children, the eldest a boy named Patrick, and his two sisters, aged ten and eight respectively. It was now approaching the hour when these three young persons would be returning from school. He decided to strike up an acquaintance with them in the street on their way home. He knew the name of the road, and as he turned the corner he saw three children of the age he was looking for making for a gate on the opposite side. He crossed the road and, addressing the boy, asked to be directed to the house of Mrs Coxon.

"Why, she lives here. What did you want to see her for?"

"Someone told me that she lets lodgings."

"She does, but she has a lodger and there's only room for one."

"What a pity!"

"Did you want to lodge with us?" asked Nora, the elder girl.

"I think it would have been nice."

"What a pity Mr Casey lives with us," piped Mary, the little one.

"Well, then there's nothing to do but for me to go to the estate office and ask them what they can do for me. Will you show me the way?"

"Of course we will," said the boy, "but we must be quick. Mother will be waiting dinner for us."

From some hidden pocket Richardson produced a box of toffee and invited his young friends to partake. Nora, who was afflicted with an oversensitive conscience, said, "Mummy wouldn't like us to eat sweets just before dinner," but she was quickly overruled by her companions. She slipped her hand into

Richardson's, saying, "I wish you could be our lodger." To this Mary added, "Mr Casey doesn't give us toffee."

"That wouldn't matter if he wasn't a beast," said the boy.

Mary became confidential. "Pat doesn't like him since he got that box on the ear."

"Why did he give him a box on the ear?"

"Because I was stalking him," said Pat defiantly.

"Why was that?"

"To see whether he went to Mrs Pomeroy's bungalow."

"I bet Ann Pomeroy put you up to that," said Nora; "you know you would do anything for her."

"You would, Pat," put in Mary. "You think that Ann is the most wonderful person in the world."

"So she is!"

"Why should Miss Pomeroy want you to stalk Mr Casey?" asked Richardson.

"Because he's a dirty sneak. But Ann didn't tell me to stalk him: she said that I must never do such a thing."

"And then of course you did it," said Nora, tossing her little head.

They had reached the estate office, and Richardson dismissed them to their dinners with well-earned thanks, inwardly recording Pat Coxon as one of the witnesses that could profitably be questioned alone when an opportunity presented itself. He was in time to catch Miss Lane in her office before she left for her midday meal. He introduced himself as a police officer from New Scotland Yard who had been sent to investigate the murder at the bungalow.

"I fear that I've called at a very inconvenient hour," he said; "you must have been on the point of closing down the office for lunch."

"That doesn't matter at all. Sit down and ask me any question you like. My lunch will have to wait, but I think I've given all the information I have to Inspector Aitkin."

"I haven't very much to ask you. I think you told Inspector Aitkin that Mr Pomeroy had intimated that he would like to dispose of the remainder of his lease. Did he come to the office to tell you this, or did you meet casually in the road or elsewhere?"

"It was quite a casual meeting when I was on the way to this office."

"What did he say?"

"I don't know that I can remember his exact words. He passed the time of day and then asked me casually whether I thought that I could find a tenant for his bungalow if he decided to leave the neighbourhood. I expressed my surprise and asked him whether his wife found it too isolated a house, as she was alone all day. He said, 'No, she likes the bungalow, but we may have to leave.'"

"I believe that when you mentioned this conversation to Mrs Pomeroy a day or two later she was surprised and told you that it was the first she had heard of it. Can you remember what she said?"

"Yes. She said, 'Oh, that's it, is it? He wants to get me away from my friends.' I didn't pursue the conversation because we were getting onto dangerous ground. You see, it was common knowledge that she had one particular friend of whom her husband disapproved."

"You mean Mr Casey?"

Miss Lane nodded meaningly. "I don't want to be mixed up in this business at all, but I might tell you confidentially, as you are a police officer, that more than once when I've been on the way to this office in the morning I have seen Mr Casey leaving the Pomeroys' bungalow after Mr Pomeroy had gone to business."

"Thank you very much, Miss Lane, and now I mustn't keep you any longer from your lunch. I may tell you that I've already had a hint of what you've told me from someone else. I'm thinking of calling on Mrs Coxon, where Casey lodges."

"You'll find her a talkative woman but not an ill-natured one. If I can be of any further use don't hesitate to come and see me again."

They parted with mutual good will. Richardson liked this kind of business-like woman with a sense of duty. She would make an excellent witness in any court of law. He stood aside to watch her lock up the office, mount her bicycle and ride away.

It was not often that he allowed the claims of the inner man to interfere with his work, but since the sacred hour of the midday meal had rendered futile all direct enquiries, he determined to follow the fashion and call at some retired eating place in Ealing to satisfy his hunger. He chose a restaurant which advertised its dining room on the first floor. The place was divided into three separate rooms with wide communication doors between them. It was crowded, but Richardson found that he was to share a table for two in the window of the third room. A harassed waitress brought the menu, which announced that Canterbury lamb with green peas was to be had. His fellow luncher at that table was in conversational mood. He listened to Richardson giving his order and remarked, "If you've ever been in New Zealand, sir, you'll know what Canterbury lamb is before it crosses the ocean in cold storage. It's a very different commodity when they haven't had to sweep the snow off it in the cold-storage chamber. It's a wonderful country, New Zealand."

"So I've heard. I suppose you know it well."

"I do. But you must never judge New Zealand from Auckland: you've got to get south before you can judge of the country."

"I've often thought that I'd like to go out there, but my profession ties me to this country."

"You ought to come out. When I come over here I wonder how anyone can stick in a little overpopulated island like this is: I miss the sense of freedom and fresh air that we have out there."

"You were born there, I suppose."

"Yes, born and bred a New Zealander. I was too young to come over for the war, otherwise I'd have joined the contingent and helped to win it."

"So you've just come over on a holiday."

"No, what brought me over was a good deal more than that. I came to see a cousin who lives in these parts. I had sad news for her—the death of a relation; it was the kind of news that it is best to give personally. It was a strange coincidence. I had come to break the news to her, and when I called at her house I found that she too was dead."

"Do you mean that she died suddenly?"

"I do. There could be no more sudden death than hers—she was murdered."

"You don't mean that it was Mrs Pomeroy?"

"Yes. I suppose that everyone in these parts has heard of the murder. 'The Bungalow Murder,' as the newspapers call it."

"Oh yes, it's been in all the papers."

"And what makes it worse is that it was the husband who did it."

"The husband has been arrested on the coroner's warrant, but nothing has been proved against him so far."

"Well, there can't be much doubt about it, can there? No one else could have any object in doing it, nor any opportunity."

Richardson looked at his fellow luncher with a new interest. He said rather coldly, "There are people who don't believe in the husband's guilt, and it's a good English maxim that a man is not to be considered guilty until the case has been proved against him. I think you said that Mrs Pomeroy was your cousin."

"Yes."

"Then I think that I ought to introduce myself. I am a police officer from New Scotland Yard, and I've been sent down here to investigate the case."

"A police officer! Don't the police believe him guilty then?"

"He hasn't been proved to be guilty."

The man laughed. "Isn't that like you police officers, always erring on the cautious side. As you are a police officer you might save me a journey to the police station by telling me when the funeral is to be. I couldn't leave without attending her funeral, could I?"

"I quite understand. If you will tell me where you are staying I will see that you receive notice of the funeral."

"I'm staying at the Palace Hotel. My name is Maddox—Edward Maddox."

Richardson took out his pencil and wrote, "Edward Maddox. Palace Hotel."

"Had your cousin any other relations in New Zealand?"

"No, only this uncle."

"Her uncle? And you came all the way from New Zealand to break the news of her uncle's death?"

"Well, yes, and to bring his will to his solicitors in Southampton Street."

"Who are they? I know most of the solicitors in Southampton Street. Some are good and some are the other thing."

"These people call themselves Jackson, Burke and Company."

"Oh, they're all right: it's an old established firm. I suppose that your cousin was her uncle's heiress?"

"Not the sole heiress." He changed the subject of the conversation rather abruptly, a fact that was not lost upon Richardson. "Will they let the husband out of prison to attend the funeral? Funny if they did."

"I can't tell you that, but I'll let you know the time and place as soon as it is decided."

They had finished their meal, and Richardson had no desire to protract their conversation. With a brief, "Well, I must be getting along," he took his leave and walked back to the villa estate, glancing once behind him to see whether he was being followed. He calculated that by this hour his new-found friends, the three Coxon children, must have returned to school and he would find their mother alone. And so he did.

She was as Miss Lane had described her, talkative but without malice. In five minutes she was entirely won over by Richardson and ready to help him in any way that lay in her power. He had presented himself as a friend of her three children—"very intelligent children, if I may say so."

"Intelligent is what they are."

"You see I am calling upon all the friends and acquaintances of the Pomeroys in the hope of getting a clear view of what led to the estrangement between Pomeroy and his wife."

"I suppose that my boy Patrick told you what he thought about the case." Richardson smiled. "I can see that he did. You see, he's quite daft about Mr Pomeroy and his cousin, Ann. He thinks there's nobody in the world like that girl Ann. You see he's mad about drawing, and she encourages him and says that there are fortunes to be made out of drawing for the newspapers, and he's just beside himself to know that Mr Pomeroy is in prison."

"Yes, all Mr Pomeroy's friends must be feeling the same about that."

"To think that such a thing should have happened here in the settlement—first the murder and then Mr Pomeroy arrested for it. Such a nice man, but you never know what people will do in a fit of temper."

"Would you say that Mr. Pomeroy had a hasty temper?"

"No, when you put it like that, I shouldn't say he had—not like my lodger, Mr. Casey, for instance. He can flare up when anything crosses him. For instance, that time when he had a quarrel with Mr Pomeroy it was Mr Casey who was saying the dreadful things and Mr Pomeroy said never a word, but just up and told him at the end never to come to his house again."

"And did he go there again?"

"Ah, there it is, you see. Men are like children. Tell them not to do a thing and the next thing you know is they're mad to do it. Just like my Nora. You tell her cake's bad for her and bread and butter is good, and it's the cake she's wanting, but on the day there's no butter in the house it's the bread and butter she's after."

"And so Mr Casey did go to the house, I suppose, when Mr Pomeroy was not at home."

"That's right, but you mustn't believe all the gossip that flies about the estate. Mrs Pomeroy, God rest her soul, was restless in this little place—found it too dull, I suppose. Many's the time she's said to me, 'I tell you, Mrs Coxon, that if something doesn't happen soon I shall be going out of my mind.' And now look what has happened. It was a judgment."

"But she had friends and relations here—Mr Pomeroy's cousin, for instance, Miss Ann."

"Well no, they weren't friends—they weren't the kind that mixes. And as for Mr Pomeroy's mother, well, I'm not one to believe in gossip, but everyone knows she wanted him to marry Ann."

"She thought that Miss Ann Pomeroy would make a more suitable wife, perhaps."

"She did, and maybe she was right. Miss Ann didn't approve of Mrs Pomeroy's friendship with Mr Casey, and she gave him a piece of her mind one day—she's an outspoken young lady, Miss Ann—and my boy Pat took his cue from her."

"And got a box on the ear for his pains."

"He did. I can see you made real friends with my children: they told you all their secrets."

"I hope we shall become better friends still," said Richardson, rising to take his leave.

Mrs Coxon followed him into the entrance hall. "Ah!" he said, "I mustn't be running away with your lodger's hat. This is mine."

Mrs Coxon laughed. "No, you've got the wrong one, but you'd have found it out if you'd tried it on. You'd never have got Mr Casey's hat onto your head: he's a smaller man than you. You can tell. That's his overcoat hanging up—it would never fit you. He's a funny man about his overcoats. Sometimes there's two or three hanging here, and sometimes they're all left up in London and he hasn't one to put on when it's raining; but there he's Irish like meself."

"I may be in this neighbourhood a little while, and I hope to see more of your children, Mrs Coxon."

"There's pleased they'll be. They talked of nothing but the gentleman who'd given them toffees."

Chapter Six

ONE OF THE most difficult tasks of the detective officer must always be to sift the grain of truth from the chaff of gossip, and as Richardson made his way to the police station in Ealing after further enquiries, he was busy sifting the modicum of grain from the mass of ill-natured scandal that was flying up and down the concrete roads of the new estate. One thing seemed to be fairly certain. The man Casey was in the habit of paying visits to the murdered woman against the wishes of her husband, and this might give some colour to the view held by some that the husband had discovered the liaison and had avenged himself on his wife. On the other hand, as far as he was able to judge, Pomeroy was not hasty or vindictive, whereas Casey might be assumed to be both, and though Casey might have more motive for killing the husband than the wife, it might well have been the act of a man subject to fits of sudden rage. At any rate there seemed to Richardson to be insufficient grounds for holding Pomeroy in prison, and it was clearly his duty to report this to his chief at Scotland Yard with the least possible delay.

He found a C.I.D. sergeant of the division on the doorstep of the police station looking up and down the road. On sight of him the man made a signal, and Richardson quickened his pace.

"There's a message just come through for you from C.O., sir. Mr Aitkin replied that you were out on an enquiry but might be expected here at any moment."

"Are they holding the line?"

"No sir, but Mr Aitkin understood that it was urgent."

Richardson ran up the steep stairs two steps at a time. Inspector Aitkin hurried out to meet him on the landing.

"The assistant commissioner himself has been on the line asking for you," he said. "I told him that you would ring up as soon as you came in. Shall I call him up?"

"Please do."

"You're through, sir," said Aitkin, putting the receiver into Richardson's hand.

"Richardson speaking, sir, from Ealing Police Station."

"I've been waiting for a report from you, Mr Richardson."

"I've been so busy with enquiries, sir, that I've had no time to write a report, but I have enough evidence to show that the man Pomeroy ought to be set at liberty."

"That is why I've had to ring you up. The coroner has been to the Home Office to report that his jury ran away with him and returned a verdict on quite insufficient evidence. The Home Office has asked me to report by telephone whether that is also the conclusion of the police."

"Yes sir, it is. I hope to let you have my report this evening."

"You might tell me now whether you have come to any conclusion about the case."

"No sir. I'm following up one or two lines of enquiry, but it is too early yet to say that I have formed any definite theory."

"Very good, Mr Richardson. Carry on, and let me have in writing only your opinion as to the innocence of Pomeroy."

"Very good, sir," replied Richardson, hanging up the receiver. He turned to Inspector Aitkin. "When Pomeroy is released where do you think he will go?"

"He won't go back to that bungalow if I know him. He'll be more likely to go to his father's house in Rosewear Road. He used to live there before he took that bungalow. Why, do you want to see him?"

"Yes, I do. You might arrange to find out whether he goes there. It's a quarter to four now. If they telephone to Brixton Prison he ought to be out early this evening, but I may not see him until tomorrow morning. I've got an enquiry to make in London, and if I want to catch them before closing I must hurry up. Putting Pomeroy out of the question, have you formed any theory about the murder?"

"There's no one else that I can see but Pomeroy, unless it was a passing tramp who came in to steal and the woman tried to stop him. To me it seems quite a motiveless murder."

"Yes, and that goes against all our training, which is to look first for the motive. That is why I'm running off to town. Quite by chance I met a man at luncheon who told me that the murdered woman had come into money, and if that is true it may alter the whole complexion of the case. I got from him the name and address of solicitors in Southampton Street who know about this legacy, and I want to catch them before they close. I shall be back again between six and seven, I hope."

As soon as Richardson was out of the building Inspector Aitkin remarked to his sergeant, "Of course, it's not for me to criticize higher authority, but we shall all look foolish if we have to rearrest Pomeroy for the murder of his wife. He could have been the only man who was on the premises at the time."

"Yes," said Sergeant Hammett. "I've thought all along that it was just a typical case of a jealous husband."

Richardson reached Southampton Street in time to find the offices of Messrs Jackson & Burke still open. The principals had gone home, but Mr Wilson, their managing clerk, received him. When Richardson exposed his business with them the clerk shook his head.

"I fear that you'll have to call tomorrow, sir," he said; "I feel that I ought not to divulge anything about this will without the sanction of my principals."

"Unless I can get some information from you, I shall have to report that the course of justice is being obstructed," observed Richardson with a smile.

"What is it that you wish to know?" asked Wilson.

"I wish to know the effect of the will which Mr Edward Maddox seems to have deposited with you."

"Oh, you mean the will of Frederick Colter, who died recently in New Zealand. He chose to have his will proved in this country, and the first steps have already been taken to obtain probate. You understand that he had property in this country as well as in New Zealand?"

"I know that Mrs Pomeroy was his heiress, but, as no doubt you have seen in the newspapers, Mrs Pomeroy is dead."

"Yes, murdered if we are to believe what the newspapers say, and as you are the officer investigating the murder I think I should be justified in giving you a resume of the will. Frederick Colter left his personal property half to his niece Stella, the wife of Miles Pomeroy, and half to his adopted son, Edward Maddox, on certain conditions. According to a codicil they were to found a training centre for young men about to emigrate to New

Zealand. He specified that Maddox should bring his will to our firm, and this he did."

"What effect would her death before the will was proved have upon the provisions of the will?"

"Mrs Pomeroy's share would go to her next of kin, who, probably, would not be legally bound to contribute towards the training centre for emigrants."

"There was no proviso in the will that in the event of her death Maddox should succeed to the whole property subject to the proviso?"

"No."

"You say that you are taking steps to obtain probate?"

"Undoubtedly probate will be obtained, when there has been time to communicate with the various beneficiaries."

"One more question. Can you give me the date when Maddox brought the will to you?"

"It was a few days ago—on the thirteenth, to be exact. He was showing a good deal of agitation. He explained that he had been down to Ealing to see his co-heiress and had found that she was dead. He said that he had called here at nine o'clock but had found that our office was not yet open. That would be so: we do not open before nine thirty."

"At what hour did he call on you the second time?"

"Just before lunch."

Richardson had found out what he wanted to know, namely, whether Maddox would benefit by the death of his co-heiress if she died before the will was proved. He would not, and so the motive that Richardson was hunting for was lacking. This line of enquiry seemed to be closed, but he had not yet finished with Ted Maddox, and, being in London, he made the Palace Hotel his next call.

At the desk there seemed to be doubts about the place where Mr Edward Maddox would be found. A page was sent round the reception rooms, calling his name as he went, and drew the first covert in the smoking room, which was decorated with a bar, and there Maddox was found gossiping with a kindred spirit. Seeing his tall visitor following the page, he came forward to shake hands and led him to a seat in the passageway, where there could be no eavesdroppers.

"Being in this neighbourhood, Mr Maddox, I called to tell you that Mr Pomeroy, the husband of that unfortunate lady, is to be released."

"Released! Why, has any fresh evidence been found to clear him?"

"I fancy it was rather the absence of evidence against him that procured his release. The coroner himself visited the Home Office expressly to obtain his release."

"Well, they always told me in New Zealand that British justice was the quickest and fairest system in the world. From the lawyer point of view that may be so, but if you ask me I should say that it was weak kneed. You have laid your hands on the only man who could have committed the crime, and then you look him over and decide that he has a nice honest face and you let him go, without finding anyone else to take his place in gaol. That's what it comes to, isn't it?"

"My particular object in calling here today, Mr Maddox, was to ask you whether you came over alone or whether any friend from New Zealand travelled with you."

The young man became alert. "I don't know the reason for your question, but I'll answer it all the same. I travelled alone in the *Aorangi*."

"I suppose you made friends on board like everyone else on a long voyage?"

"Well, I couldn't take my exercise on deck with a gag on."

"Exactly, and you were an object of some interest, no doubt—a young man who has inherited a considerable fortune does not go unnoticed."

"If you mean that I bragged about it, you're wrong. I may have mentioned it to one or two, but I can't see what that has to do with you."

Richardson decided quickly that, he must seek his information rather from the ship's officers than from the young man himself, but he was sure from the resentful tone that he had evoked unpleasant memories of the voyage.

"I'm sorry if I seem to have asked too many questions, but I'm only complying with my instructions. I won't take up any more of your time."

It was but a step from the hotel to the steamboat office, where he learned that the captain of the *Aorangi* was at home on leave for a few days, but that the purser of the boat happened to be in the office at that moment, if Richardson would like to see him. The clerk carried the official visiting card into a room behind the counter and emerged almost instantly to invite Richardson to follow him.

He found two men in this room: the one seated at a mahogany writing table, clearly one of the superior officers of the company; the other a weather-beaten man of between thirty and forty—obviously the purser. The manager at the writing table received his visitor cordially and glanced at his card.

"This gentleman," he said, "is the purser of the *Aorangi*, but if your business is of the usual kind I hope that you'll allow me to be present. Confidence men have a special interest for me. I don't know which I admire more, their flair for the possible victim, or their power of acting. The part I should like to see played is that of the old Irishman who has come into an unexpected fortune. Please sit down."

"It is not confidence men this time, Mr Drury. I want to get some information about a passenger named Edward Maddox, who travelled from New Zealand." The purser's expression at the mention of the name was instructive; it called forth memories.

"That young man was a card. When he first came on board he had come into a little money; but as the voyage continued the fortune grew and grew, until we found that we had a real live millionaire to deal with, and I can tell you that the men, from the chief steward downward, were badly disappointed when he slipped ten bob into their hands."

"Did he make any friends on board?"

"Oh, just the usual type that one meets on board ship who hang round passengers reputed to be rich."

"You don't mean the ordinary confidence man?"

"No, for a wonder we had none of them on board. But there was one flashy-looking card who stuck pretty close to Maddox; in fact, they left the ship together."

"Name of Otway?"

"Yes, but how did you know that?"

"It was only a guess. When I call at a hotel about anyone I always ask for the register and make a note of the name preceding and following that of the person I'm enquiring about."

"Then Otway is staying at the Palace, and you may be sure that Maddox is footing the bill. Otway never paid for anything on board; he always got his pal to stand him what he wanted."

"I suppose you can't give me any special information about Otway?"

"All I can tell you is that he booked his ticket at Wellington, and unless there's any special reason, we don't ask any questions. I do remember one thing, however. This fellow Otway came down on the morning we sailed to have a look at his cabin. I'd given him the upper berth. When he went down the gangway he was stopped by a police officer in plain clothes. I didn't overhear what they said, but when I asked the policeman afterwards what it was all about, he said that it was only to know whether Otway was leaving the country. Very evasive he was, like they always are in New Zealand."

Richardson had one more visit to make before he returned to Ealing. When Charles Morden had given him his instructions he had said with a dry smile, "You may not be surprised when I tell you that you owe this job to an old friend. You can guess whom I mean—Mr Milsom. He may be an important witness in the case because he was actually present when the body was discovered."

It was to Jim Milsom that he paid his next visit. He guessed that at this hour Milsom would be found either at his club or at his flat. He chose the flat, for after the dull yet exacting routine of a publisher's office he judged that repose was what the doctor would order. He was right. The door of the flat had scarcely closed upon him when he heard the clink of a decanter on glass.

"You're just in time for a spot of sherry, my friend, and by the look of you, you need it badly. Sleuthing must always be dry work, but to a trained sleuth like you it must dry every inch of the oesophagus, if that is what the anatomists call the bally pipe through which you take your nourishment. Say the word: sherry or a whisky and soda?"

"A very small glass of sherry, thank you."

"Tut tut! When these glasses are full to the brim they scarcely hold enough to drown a mosquito."

"I was not quite sure whether you were still in the publishing business, Mr Milsom."

"What do you take me for? When I gave my word to my uncle that I'd stick to the job I stuck to it. Of course I don't pretend to publish *belles-lettres* or that kind of tripe. Detective fiction is my line, and there I can claim to be a judge. I can tell you that no one is more surprised than my uncle to find that I'm sticking to it. What he doesn't know is that when I read the manuscript of a thriller a sort of halo of light glows about the guilty man at his first entry in chapter three —it's natural intuition."

"How is your uncle?"

"The old boy's in the pink, and so is that young rascal Geoffrey, who's been entered for Rugby, if you please. But you didn't come here to talk about the old boy. I've been expecting you for days to tell me how you're getting on with that case in Ealing."

"Well, Pomeroy is being released this evening."

"High time, too. If they'd delayed it another day I'd have heaved a brick through the window of the Home Office as the suffragettes used to do when they were peeved."

"You felt sure from the first, then, that Pomeroy was innocent?"

"I would have staked my life on it. You had only to see the poor devil. He had a hell of a time from that wife of his, but if all the husbands in the country who are nagged by their wives resorted to cracking them on the head in the bathroom, there wouldn't be prisons enough to hold them."

"As you know, I did not take over the case until the third day after the murder. You seem to have been in the house from the beginning. What I want is a detailed account from you giving me exactly what happened."

Richardson listened intently to his friend's statement, jotting down a note or two in pencil while he talked. He could not help admiring the power of vivid narrative which Milsom displayed.

"There!" said the narrator. "I believe that I've coughed up everything, and with you sitting glaring at me without winking for ten minutes I think I've earned another sherry. But surely your sleuths have found out if any stranger was on the estate that morning?"

"That's not so easy as it sounds. The main road into Ealing runs along the back of the estate, and hundreds of cars go past from daylight till long after dark. Even a car parked at the roadside might pass unnoticed for an hour or more."

"And of course your inspector Aitkin started off all wrong from the first by thinking that it was Pomeroy. Now tell me your own views."

Richardson had a natural respect for the intelligence of his friend Milsom, and knew that he could be trusted to be discreet. He related briefly the result of his enquiries up to this point. Milsom listened attentively and at the end clapped his detective friend on the knee, saying, "Otway's your man. Follow him up for all you are worth."

"I mean to find out something more about him," said Richardson.

Chapter Seven

"THE MOMENT is now come for me to make a confession," said Milsom. "When those doctor-men's eyes were glistening with stupidity on the morning the body was found, and they were insisting that no one should leave the house on pain of incarceration in a police cell, I slipped out to the car to get my cigarette case, and, cuddling up to the bottom step of that bungalow, I found this." He moved to his writing table and took from the drawer an envelope containing the stub of a cigar.

"But this may have been thrown down by one of the doctors as he entered the house."

"That is what I thought, but this was dead and cold. It must have been lying there for hours after life became extinct."

"You ought to have handed this over to the police long ago."

"No doubt I ought, but as I've already hinted to you, I thought your inspector Aitkin a prize idiot: that is what determined me to keep it for you. I carried the corpse to a tobacconist in whom I have confidence. He conducted a careful post-mortem and pronounced the defunct to have been rolled in Havana to the pleasing drone of a Spanish thriller read aloud to some hundreds of workmen as they rolled and pasted the tobacco leaves. I went even further. I buttonholed each of those medical men and offered them a cigar. This little civility was a pleasing illustration of character. Dr Green grinned, raised his hand to put the temptation aside and said that he'd never smoked one in his life. Dr Leach looked regretful, but said that if he came in smelling of cigar smoke, sooner or later he would lose his job. Therefore, I argued, this was an unknown person, probably the miscreant himself."

"What about Pomeroy? He had been to a bridge party the night before. Cigars would certainly have been included among the refreshments."

"Not cigars rolled in Havana, my dear sir. I know the brand that pass for cigars in Ealing—tuppence is what they cost, but you can purchase them for even less. They look like cigars when viewed from a distance; it is only when you come to use the senses of touch and smell that you recognize them for what they are."

"Still, you can't say positively that Pomeroy didn't have a good cigar offered to him that night. It is all your conjecture. If it was left by the murderer it proves that he wasn't a common tramp who had strayed off the high road; neither was he very well known to Mrs Pomeroy, otherwise he would not have sacrificed a good two and a half inches of his smoke by throwing it away before he went in."

"You see, my friend, it's always worth coming to me when you're in a difficulty. I provide you with a clue while you wait. To my mind that's another strand in the rope that will dangle Otway, who is just the kind of bloke who would smoke a good cigar at the expense of a fellow traveller."

"You're going a little too fast for me. Granted that Otway had a police record in New Zealand; that he hung onto Maddox and learned that the dead woman was to share a legacy with him—but for the life of me I can't see how that can be construed into a motive for killing her."

"When you burrow a little further into the case you'll find the motive all right." Richardson had risen. "You're not going?"

"Indeed I am. I ought to have been back in Ealing an hour ago. I'm going to see Pomeroy, who will have had time to get to his father's house by now."

"You'll ring me up and tell me the result of your interview with him?"

"I can't promise to do that, but I daresay I'll be seeing you again soon."

"Well, do try and find something for me to do in this case. It's ages since I did any sleuthing, and I'm getting cold in the collar."

The house of Pomeroy's father had been pointed out to Richardson. It was a prewar construction of the ordinary suburban type—ugly, solidly built and comfortable. The class that lived in these houses was often referred to as the backbone of the country; it consisted of unadventurous people who lived regular lives, paying their way with some difficulty, but departing this life without owing a penny even to the rating authority. Ann Pomeroy herself opened the door in answer to Richardson's ring. She switched on the hall light in order to recognize her visitor.

"I wondered who it was," she said. "You've come at a rather emotional moment. My cousin Miles has just come home, and naturally my aunt and uncle are very much moved. Come into my den and tell me what I can do for you."

She took him into a little room opening out of the hall. Richardson noticed that there were pictures and flowers wherever there was room for them; that it was walled with bookshelves; that the writing table was just such as one would expect in the den of a woman who wrote. Ann Pomeroy was a type new to him.

"Sit down, Mr Richardson, and tell me how I can help you."

"I'm afraid you cannot. My only object in calling was to see Mr Miles Pomeroy as soon as he was liberated."

"I can bring him in here to see you, but my aunt and uncle are not in a fit state to receive visitors. I could leave you here together."

"Thank you very much. I will wait here."

He heard her light step on the tiled floor; heard her open a door of what must be the sitting room; heard her close it softly behind her and the hum of voices from within. Then the door opened, and he heard a man's step crossing the hall. He rose as Miles Pomeroy came in, and noted the ravages that his misfortune had worked in his face.

"I am Superintendent Richardson," he said. "I should not have troubled you to see me at such a moment had it not been for the necessity for clearing you entirely from any suspicion. Shall we sit down?"

"I will answer any question you put to me, though I've told the whole story more than once."

"I'm not going to worry you by asking you to tell it again. All that you have told the police has been verified. My object in seeing you is to ask a few questions about your late wife's relations. I understand that she had an uncle living in New Zealand."

"Yes, a Mr Colter, a sheep farmer near Wellington. I'd quite forgotten until you reminded me of it that on the morning of my wife's death a young man called at the bungalow to say that the uncle was dead. He said he was the adopted son of Mr Colter."

"I gather that you had never seen him before."

"No."

"Had you ever seen the uncle, Mr Colter?"

"No, I've never been to New Zealand."

"And Mr Colter never came to England?"

"Yes, he had paid more than one visit to London, but my wife lived with him in New Zealand for some years. She came over to study for the stage."

"Did she ever get an engagement?"

"No, she married me instead."

"Has she any relations in England?"

"Yes—a brother, but as far as I know there had been no communication between the two of late years."

"She knew Ted Maddox, of course?"

"Yes. He was the son of a neighbouring sheep farmer, and Colter adopted him with the view of making him his manager and afterwards, perhaps, his heir. My wife used to say that when her uncle died it would be found that he had left everything to this boy and had forgotten her altogether. He had never really forgiven her for coming to England to train for the stage."

"I suppose that Maddox was younger than your wife?"

"Yes, five or six years younger."

"Were they good friends, do you know?"

"We did not often talk of him, but on the rare occasions when he was mentioned she said that he was on his good behaviour at first, but that it was not long before he began to give himself airs and to regard himself as the future heir to the old man. This had something to do with her becoming restless and wanting to leave New Zealand."

"Do you know whether she had heard from her uncle recently?"

"She never showed me her letters. Occasionally I noticed a letter with the New Zealand stamp, but I never questioned her about it, because I noticed that it always made her more irritable than usual."

"Where did she keep her letters?"

"In a locked suitcase."

"Do you know whether the police opened the suitcase when they made their search?"

"I don't know what they did after my arrest," he answered bitterly.

"Have you a telephone in the house?"

"Yes, my cousin has one; it is just behind you on her desk."

"Would she allow me to use it, do you think?"

"Of course she would."

Richardson swung round and asked for Ealing Police Station. The answer came at once.

"Ealing police speaking."

"Can I speak to Inspector Aitkin?"

"Hold on a minute." He heard the retreating footsteps, followed by the sound of heavy boots approaching the instrument. "Inspector Aitkin, C.I.D., speaking."

"Superintendent Richardson here. When you searched the Pomeroy bungalow, did you open a locked suitcase in the bedroom?"

"No sir. It was marked with the initials of the dead woman, and I thought that it contained only female wearing apparel."

"That's a pity, but still you have the keys of the house still, so it's not too late."

"Yes, they're here waiting for Pomeroy to call for them."

"Good! Then please go round to the bungalow, take that locked suitcase and bring it to me here. I'm speaking from Mr Pomeroy senior's house, and Mr Pomeroy is with me. You know the address?"

"Oh yes. I'll bring the suitcase right away."

At that moment the door opened to admit Ann Pomeroy.

"I must apologize for using your telephone, Miss Pomeroy," said Richardson.

"I didn't come about that: I came to see whether you had not asked all the questions you want to, because I think that my cousin has had about enough for today."

Richardson smiled. "I think that you may safely leave that to me, Miss Pomeroy. I'm not in the habit of using what they call the third degree with people whom I question."

Pomeroy gave her a wan but reassuring look. "We are getting on very well together, Ann. We've sent for Stella's suitcase to look at her correspondence."

Ann drew herself up. "I can tell you in advance what you'll find—correspondence which proves my theory to be correct."

"You mean...?"

"That the suitcase is packed with love letters from that man Casey. I'm sorry to hurt your feelings, Miles, but things have become so desperate that we have to face facts."

"I think that you had better be here when we open the suitcase, Miss Pomeroy. It ought to be here in a few minutes."

"While we are waiting I'm going to bring in some coffee and sandwiches. I'm sure that you must be hungry, Miles."

She hurried away before her cousin could protest and returned bearing a tray which must have been prepared in advance, since she returned almost instantly. To please her Miles Pomeroy felt that he could not decline the sandwiches and was surprised to find himself eating with appetite, and insisted on Richardson sharing the meal with him. They even reached the point of discussing the news in the evening paper. Miles Pomeroy, a keen Conservative, was launching out upon the political news when Richardson reminded him with a smile that, whatever they might feel inwardly, police officers had no politics, except, perhaps, at the moment of a general election.

The front-door bell rang, and Miles went out to open it; he returned carrying the suitcase for which they had been waiting.

He signalled to Richardson to go to the front door, where he found Detective Inspector Aitkin standing.

"Where's the key?" he asked.

"We never found the key, sir. If the dead woman had one, she must have hidden it away in some unexpected place; we've searched the house for it."

"I suppose you could find a locksmith?"

"Yes sir, but if the woman died intestate and without children, the husband would succeed to all her property and would have a right to break it open."

"Quite right, but we shall have to ask for his assent first. Come in, so that you can serve as a witness to what passes."

He brought Aitkin into the room and presented him to Pomeroy and his cousin. "Do you know, Mr Pomeroy, whether your wife ever made a will?"

"No, I'm sure that she didn't. When I made mine I suggested that she should do the same, but she laughed and said, 'I've nothing to leave; why go to the expense and bother of making a will?"

"Then you have the right to open this suitcase as her next of kin: it belongs to you."

"Very well, break it open."

The breaking of the trumpery fastening was the matter of a few seconds. It was a fitted dressing case, which accounted for its weight, but the space left for clothing was packed with letters.

"Will you want me any longer?" asked Aitkin.

"No, you have plenty to do: I'll ring you up if I find that you are wanted."

The dead woman was one of those who put letters back into their envelopes, and therefore the task of sorting them out was an easy one. Richardson selected five envelopes bearing a New Zealand stamp and postmark. The most numerous of these hoarded letters bore the Ealing postmark, and these he tossed aside for future examination.

"Have I your permission to read these letters from New Zealand?" he asked Pomeroy.

"Certainly."

Reading them, Richardson realized why Stella Pomeroy had never received a letter from her uncle without showing irritation. They were cool letters, such as an uncle might write from a sense of duty, but they always terminated in eulogies of his adopted son, Ted Maddox, who had succeeded in making himself indispensable. Behind this lay the inference that Ted had the interest of his adopted father at heart, while she had deserted him.

Pomeroy had been glancing through a number of letters with the London postmark. They were all the same—refusals of engagements in theatrical companies. He tossed one of them over to Richardson.

"She hoarded these letters and read them over from time to time, although they made her bitter."

Ann Pomeroy had been silently looking through the letters bearing an Ealing postmark.

"I see you are helping us, Miss Pomeroy," said Richardson.

"Not because I like it: these letters make me sick. As I expected they are all written by the same man. It's the dates I'm looking at. Here, at last, is the latest, written on September twelfth, the day before the murder. You don't want to see it, I suppose, Miles," she said as she passed the letter to Richardson, who glanced through it.

It was an impassioned love letter of a man who knew something of the art of love making. The last sentences in the missive interested Richardson.

We shall have to find another hour for my visits. They have made me exchange duties with Kane from the 14th, which means that I must travel up by the same train as the Nuisance. What hour do you suggest?

Ann laid her hand on her cousin's sleeve. "I think that you had better go back to Aunt, or she will wonder what has become of you." She led him to the door and closed it behind him; then she came hack to Richardson, her eyes shining with triumph.

"You see, I was right. That man Casey was Stella's lover; he did call at that hour in the morning when her husband had left for town. He was to change his hours of duty on the fourteenth, therefore it is almost certain that he called on the thirteenth to make new arrangements. There must have been a sudden quarrel."

"I can't allow myself the luxury of jumping to conclusions, Miss Pomeroy. I must go away and think things over, but I am infinitely obliged both to you and Mr Pomeroy for the help you have given me."

Chapter Eight

IT WAS LATE in the evening when Richardson found himself mounting the stairs to Inspector Aitkin's room at the police station. Detective inspectors, whether competent or otherwise, can lay no claim to regular hours of duty, and so, as Richardson expected, he found Aitkin in his room.

"You've been busy this evening, sir. Did you get any result from those letters?"

"I did, and it's that that has brought me here so late. There were letters in that suitcase that pointed strongly to a man named Casey having been on compromising terms with Mrs

Pomeroy. Do you know the man? He lodges with a Mrs Coxon and is a journalist."

"Oh yes, everybody on the estate knows Casey. He's the sort of Irishman who takes a delight in rubbing people up the wrong way. He comes over here to make his living and never stops running this country down and boosting his own poor little island. He's a hasty-tempered little devil, and he's had to defend himself with his fists more than once."

"Well, among those letters we found some that proved that he used to call on Mrs Pomeroy at the very hour at which the murder must have been committed that morning."

"Come, come! That's serious. Wouldn't we be justified in sending for him and putting him through the hoop?"

"I think we'll have to see him on some excuse or other, but we must be careful about how we do it: we don't want to have another mistaken arrest."

"Did you find any begging letters from one of the dead woman's actor friends asking for cast-off clothing?"

"No, no begging letter of any kind."

"Well, until we have evidence of where Pomeroy's raincoat went to, it will take a good deal to persuade me that his arrest was mistaken."

"According to those letters Casey now has to catch the same morning train as Miles Pomeroy."

"That would be the eight thirty, so if we are to see him we'd better lose no time but see him tonight. Shall I have him brought down here?"

"Yes, I suppose that will be better than seeing him in a house with a lot of children, but will he come unless you let him think that he's under arrest?"

"Oh yes. If I go, he'll come all right. He's not one who would like to get into the bad books of the police."

"You'd better take my car to save time. While you're gone I'll draft out my report on the case."

Richardson's pen travelled rapidly over the paper; his reports were always regarded by his colleagues at headquarters as marvels of clear narration. He was surprised to find how quickly Inspector Aitkin had accomplished his mission when he heard his voice on the stairs.

"You'll find them a little steep, Mr Casey. I think we shall find the superintendent in this room."

The door was flung open. Inspector Aitkin cried, "Mr Dennis Casey, sir."

The new arrival was a slim Irishman with wavy dark hair and good eyes and teeth. There was nothing about his manner to show that he resented being brought down to be questioned, or that he feared the result of the interrogation. He was quite at his ease. Richardson opened the conversation at once.

"Sit down, Mr Casey. In the course of my enquiry into the death of Mrs Stella Pomeroy at the bungalow, it has come to my knowledge that you were in the habit of calling upon her at a rather early hour—eight thirty, to be precise."

"Eight forty-five, to be more precise still."

"Well, we'll say eight forty-five. That was after her husband had left for the station."

"That's quite correct. That was the most convenient hour both for her and for me."

"That was the hour at which the unfortunate woman met her death on the thirteenth."

"Then I suppose that it is fortunate for me to be able to prove that I was not there on that day."

"Very fortunate, if you can prove it."

Casey's manner changed. "I've told you that I can prove it, but I'm not called upon to do so at the bidding of a policeman, for all that he is dressed in plain clothes. Bring your charge of murder against me, and I'll make you look foolish for the second time in this case. First it was Pomeroy that you had to release. I am number two, and I suppose when you have to drop me you'll bring in a third guilty man. What a case it will make for the newspapermen in Fleet Street."

"You are not helping us, Mr Casey. We happen to know that the dead woman was a very intimate friend of yours. Surely you have a strong motive for desiring to see her murderer brought to justice."

"I see what has happened. Even the poor girl's private correspondence is not sacred from the eyes of the police. I don't envy you your job, Mr.—I didn't catch your name."

Richardson pursued his questions without noticing the last remark. "You were changing the hour for your visit on the fourteenth. This was to be your last visit, eight forty-five on the thirteenth."

"I have told you that I did not go on the thirteenth, and at the proper time I shall have witnesses to prove it."

"When did you first hear of the death of Mrs Pomeroy?"

"At about one-thirty the same day: it came through the wire at the office."

"And it was a bad shock to you?"

"Well, of course it was." For the first time Richardson detected a trace of emotion in Casey's features.

"As you were not changing your hours until the fourteenth, why didn't you go on the thirteenth, according to your practice? You see we've not yet found any trace of a stranger being near the house on the morning of the thirteenth, and we thought that you might be able to help us."

"I've told you already that I didn't go to the bungalow that morning."

"You may as well tell me why not. You don't want to make the case any more obscure than it is."

"Very well, I'll tell you. I was coming towards the bungalow when I caught sight of Pomeroy, in a disreputable suit of old clothes, making for the town. It meant, of course, that he was not going to business that morning, so I followed him to see what he was going to do. He went into a fruiterer's and came out with a parcel, then to a tobacconist's and newspaper shop, and then he turned for home. I realized that it would be no good for me to call at the house that morning, and so I went to the station and caught an earlier train. This I can prove."

"Thank you very much, Mr Casey. That is all I need trouble you with this evening."

When the man's footsteps had died away Aitkin broke out reproachfully, "You never made him try on that raincoat, sir. I had it here, all ready."

"No, I could not have forced him to put it on if he'd objected, which he would have done. The story he tells is quite a likely one, and we have no evidence that would contradict it."

"Then if Casey wasn't at the house and we can hear of no stranger who was, I shall feel, as I always have felt, that we did wrong in not holding onto Pomeroy." Richardson pulled out his diary. "I see that on the thirteenth it was fine and sunny in the morning. Casey wouldn't have been wearing a raincoat, and, according to his story, Pomeroy was wearing what looked like a suit of cast-off clothes for working in his garden."

"I have it! Quite a number of men stick on an old raincoat instead of a dressing gown over their pajamas to go to the bathroom. I'll go to the bungalow in the morning and see whether Pomeroy has a dressing gown. If not he might very well have been wearing that raincoat that's in the other room."

"That's possible, but we can do no more tonight." As Richardson's footsteps died away on the stairs Aitkin's spirits rose: he felt that he had scored the last point. His triumph was to be short-lived. He heard footsteps returning up the stairs. It was Richardson with one of his interminable questions.

"Didn't you tell me that you had examined all the male clothing in that bungalow without finding bloodstains on any of the garments? Surely you must remember whether there was a dressing gown."

"Yes sir, there was—an affair in blue silk with a silk cord round the waist. It did not look as if it was used every day— seemed to be kept for state occasions, and it was right at the back of the wardrobe."

"Well, I'll leave the question of the dressing gown to you when you see Pomeroy in the morning."

"I'll make it my first job," said Aitkin.

True to his word he was at the bungalow early next morning. Pomeroy not having returned from his father's house, the police were still in possession of the key.

Aitkin let himself in and went into Pomeroy's dressing room to make a second survey of his clothing. His recollection had been accurate. The blue silk dressing gown was hanging in its place at the back of the wardrobe. This was to be the day of the funeral of the murdered woman. Surely, thought Aitkin, the husband would attend and would require a black coat and tie such as were hanging in the wardrobe. Would he come down in person for the clothes or send for them? He decided that he was not called upon to wait on the chance of someone coming; he would go to the father's house.

When he rang the bell it was Ann Pomeroy who came to the door. "Ah, it's you, Inspector. What can I do for you?"

"I called to see Mr Miles Pomeroy, as I still have the key of his bungalow and he may want some clothing from it for the funeral today."

"Mr Pomeroy is ill in bed, and the doctor won't let him attend the funeral."

"Is it anything serious?"

"After what he's gone through it's not surprising that he's had a reaction and that he doesn't feel equal to seeing police officers. I can take the key and give it to him."

"Well, I wanted to ask him a question."

"I'll take any message to him, but I cannot let you see him."

"It's quite a small question—to ask him what he was in the habit of wearing when he went to the bathroom."

On her way up to her cousin's room Ann puzzled over the question. She decided to be diplomatic and not to worry him needlessly by saying that the police were at the door. She upped to be sure that he was awake and then went in and put her question.

"Would you like me to go down to the bungalow and bring up any clothes—a dressing gown, for instance?"

"The dressing gown doesn't matter particularly, but I'd like some other things if you're going down—clean pajamas, and so forth."

"Not a dressing gown? What do you wear when you go to the bathroom?"

"I don't bother to put on anything over my pajama except in the winter."

"All right. I'll go down and get some things this morning."

She went back to the front door, and Aitkin rose from his seat in the hall.

"My cousin says he wears nothing over his pajamas when he goes to the bathroom, so your surmise that he was wearing that bloodstained coat is wrong."

"You are jumping rather quickly to conclusions, Miss Pomeroy."

"The minds of police officers are not difficult to read."

"We police officers have to do our duty and must leave no stone unturned in doing it."

"And I, as Mr Pomeroy's cousin, intend to leave no stone unturned in finding out to whom his raincoat—which you believe to be that bloodstained coat that you found—was sent."

Though Ann had spoken so confidently about tracing her cousin's coat, she was not feeling very confident as she returned to her den. She had questioned Miles, but he knew nothing—neither addresses or names of any of these actor friends who had sponged upon his wife. Apparently the dead woman had used her husband's wardrobe as a supply depot for her impecunious friends, and the matter was only referred to between the couple when Miles missed a garment that he was attached to. Ann was still musing when the front-door bell rang again. She went to it to find a tall and rather seedy-looking man, whose chin needed the attention of a razor. His features seemed vaguely familiar to her.

"I have called to see Mr Miles Pomeroy," he said.

"I'm afraid that no one can see him: he is ill in bed."

"But I am his dead wife's brother. I read of her death in the paper."

"Please come in. I am Miles' cousin. We can talk quietly in here," she said, leading him into her den and closing the door. "I'm afraid that what you saw in the newspapers must have been a shock to you."

"Yes," he agreed. "The manner of her death was so tragic."

Ann had been looking at him with curiosity. It was a weak face with marks of self-indulgence upon it—clearly a man of no strength of will—and yet it was not in any way a repulsive face. Ann resolved to take him into her confidence.

"Have you heard that the funeral is to take place today—at three o'clock, I believe."

"I should like to attend. Where does the procession start from?"

"From the mortuary. Anyone will tell you where that is, or better still, you had better stay and lunch here and go to the funeral with my uncle."

"That's very kind of you, but shan't I be in the way?"

"Of course not. At moments like this families must cling together."

"I was shocked when I saw that her husband had been arrested: it was a preposterous thing to do."

"Have you ever met Miles?"

"Yes, at their wedding. I gave my sister away."

Ann had been abroad at the time of her cousin's wedding, and his parents had never discussed the marriage with her.

"It was a preposterous thing," she said; "and what is worse, the police, or some of them, still believe that he was guilty."

"But surely his innocence has been fully established by this time."

"Yes, to all sensible people, but one cannot always include individual policemen in that description. I wonder if you could help me over one thing."

"If I possibly can, I will. What is it?"

"Well, you will have read that a bloodstained raincoat was found hidden near the house, which was presumed to have been worn by the murderer. Some of the police are trying to prove that it is my cousin's coat. He swears it is not. He had one like it, but his wife gave it away some weeks ago. Unfortunately he doesn't know whom she gave it to. Did she by any chance send it to you?"

"No, I haven't heard from her for years, and certainly I never asked her for a coat."

"According to Miles she used to get begging letters from actors who had been unlucky on the stage. Do you know the names of any of her friends of that kind?"

"Well, I know one or two men in the profession who might do such a thing. I could give you their names, but I don't know their addresses."

"Well, their names might be of some use."

"Clement Wickham—she knew him—and Arthur Rowton."

Ann went to her writing desk and made a note of the names. "You've no idea at all where one could find them?"

"I might be able to find out. I heard that Clement was going to tour the North with a company, but Rowton I haven't heard of for six months. I'll see what I can do and send you any information I can get hold of."

"I should be grateful. Now I'll go and tell Aunt and Uncle that you are here."

Chapter Nine

RICHARDSON had a friend in London—a friend who was very commonly called by the police as an expert witness on bloodstains and by dint of frequent appearance for the prosecution had established himself in the criminal courts and the estimation of the public as an authority whose opinion could not be gainsaid.

When Richardson handed in his first report on the case suggesting that the bloodstained coat should be handed over to Dr Manson for report, which suggestion had been approved, he had himself taken it to Wimpole Street. He was not surprised when a telephone message was handed to him requesting that he should himself go round to receive the expert's report. He called at the house in Wimpole Street, and, after explaining the object of his visit to the maid, she returned with a message that the doctor himself desired to see him.

"Well, here is the coat and here is my report, Mr Richardson, but one point that I have not included in the report may or may not be of interest to you, as it cannot appear in my report unless it is elicited by counsel in examination. It is this. I judge from these bloodstains that the coat was worn by the victim of the assault and not by the assailant."

"Indeed, Doctor, that is a very important point. I scarcely like to ask you how you came to that conclusion."

"That is not a very easy point to answer. It is by the position of the bloodstains. The blood has run down from the scalp to the collar and so on down the coat. You will not have to call me as a witness as to that: the practitioner who saw the body would himself agree. If the assailant had been wearing this coat and blood had spurted onto it, I should have expected quite a different disposition of the bloodstains. You might bear this in mind in your further investigations."

"You know, of course, Doctor, that the murdered woman had bled a great deal. Her body was found in the bath, and her dressing gown, which apparently she was wearing when the blow was struck, was pretty well drenched in blood."

"Then how does the question of this raincoat strike you?"

"That it can scarcely belong to this case at all, if it was the coat of a victim and not an assailant."

"Exactly. You may go to the top of the class. I am telling you this because I think it may help you in your investigation."

"Thank you, Doctor, but I fear that this is going to make my enquiry even more difficult. The assailant has not yet been traced, although he must have been more or less covered with blood."

"That's a very common fallacy. In more cases than not the clothing worn by persons guilty of wounding, particularly when a blunt instrument has been used, has been found free from bloodstains altogether, or bearing only small spots. There is the well-known case of Gardner, whose throat was cut, and yet no blood-stains at all were found on the clothing of the man who was convicted of the murder. I wish that every police officer realized this, for many are led to magnify stains of red paint and rust on the clothing of a suspected person into bloodstains."

"In this case you think that the woman may have been killed without any of her blood spurting onto the assailant's clothing?"

"Everything depends upon the relative position of the two persons. A murderer may attack his victim from behind and cut the throat to simulate suicide. In this case we cannot tell whether the blow was struck from behind, from the front or from either side, but in no case is it safe to assume that blood will be found on the assailant's clothing from a blow on the head."

"Well, Doctor, I confess that what you have said is a little embarrassing. You know, of course, that the husband was arrested on the coroner's warrant and subsequently released largely because there was no circumstantial evidence of bloodstains on his clothing."

"Did you never hear of the murder of Glasse in Ireland in 1873? In that case there were no bloodstains on the assailant's clothing, though the wounds on the head of the murdered man had been produced by a blunt weapon. In that case the prisoner was tried three times —the first two the jury disagreed since there was no blood on his clothes. On the third trial he was convicted, and this was followed by his confession of guilt. He said that there had been small stains on his clothing, but that he had known enough about blood to remove these with cold water before they had had time to dry."

"But in this case, Doctor, the assailant had lifted the woman into the bath, and his clothing ought to have been drenched with blood."

Dr Manson paused in thought. "Supposing that he dammed up the source of bleeding with the dressing gown before he lifted her body into the bath..."

"You've given me a lot to think about, Doctor. I shall go back and start again with all I've learned from you to help me."

This was the day and hour of the funeral. Richardson left Dr Manson and directed his driver to make for Ealing Cemetery. He had plenty to think about: Who, other than the husband, had the interest or the opportunity for committing the crime, and, if it should be afterwards discovered in official quarters that he had acted precipitately in urging Miles Pomeroy's release, it would be good-bye to the reputation that he had so patiently been building up. The strongest point in Pomeroy's favour—that his clothing had been free from bloodstains—had now been blotted out by the expert explanation of Dr Manson. True, Milsom—for whose common sense he had a great respect and who had seen Pomeroy both just before and after the discovery of the body— had been convinced that the man was not acting a part.

There can be no sadder or more dreary ceremony than the last rites of a murdered woman without friends. The husband, of course, should have been present, but he was ill in bed and his wife had failed to make friends among her neighbours, and in fact had quarrelled with several that she did know. Richardson arrived too late for the funeral procession, but there was no difficulty in finding the position of the grave in the cemetery from the vast crowd of curious onlookers that had collected. Many of them would explain their presence by saying, "Well, it might have been me." Close to the grave he saw an old man, the chief mourner, whom he guessed to be Pomeroy's father; with him was a seedily dressed person unknown to Richardson. The only other mourner was Edward Maddox. On the outskirts of the crowd he recognized Ann Pomeroy and made towards her.

"Your cousin isn't here," he said in a low voice.

"No, he is ill in bed, and the doctor would not hear of letting him come out."

"Nothing serious, I hope."

"Nervous exhaustion, the doctor said it is."

"Am I right in guessing that the elderly gentleman standing by the grave is Mr Pomeroy's father?"

"Yes; and do you know who the man with him is?"

"No."

"He is the dead woman's brother."

"Indeed. What is his profession?"

"He is an actor, but I fancy an actor without an engagement. If you would like to speak to him afterwards I will bring him up and introduce him."

"Yes, I would like to speak to him. You know, of course, who the third man is?"

"No. I've been wondering."

"He is the adopted son of the uncle who died in New Zealand—Edward Maddox."

"I wonder why he came to the funeral? Ah, they're moving off. I'll go and fetch Mr Grant, if you'll wait here."

But before Ann returned, Edward Maddox made his way towards Richardson. He shook hands.

"I'm glad you were able to let me know about the funeral. Doesn't it strike you as a curious thing that the husband shouldn't be here?"

"I understand that he is ill in bed," replied Richardson coldly; "but this is her brother coming towards us now. Do you know him?"

"What, Arthur Grant?" He went forward to meet the newcomer. "Do you remember me? I'm Ted Maddox. I shouldn't have known you: you have changed."

"You were only a boy when I left New Zealand."

"You don't look as if things have been prospering with you. You know that Colter is dead and has left everything to Stella and me? Poor girl, she won't want hers, but I'll see that you are all right. Come straight back with me now to my hotel and tell me all about yourself."

Grant allowed himself to be led away, and Richardson did not try to stop him.

"You've let him go without asking him any questions," said Ann reproachfully.

"It doesn't matter. I can call at Maddox's hotel."

"Mr Grant is going to put me in touch with the man who may have had that raincoat given to him. When I can clear that up, the police can have no further suspicions against Miles."

Richardson did not think it worth while to tell her that the raincoat had ceased to have any significance. He was concerned now with the half-smoked cigar which Milsom had picked up at the door of the bungalow. He was anxious to satisfy himself whether or no it could have been Pomeroy who had left it there.

"Can you give me the address of that Mrs Trefusis who gave evidence at the inquest?"

Ann looked surprised at this unexpected question, but she had long ceased to marvel at the working of the police mind. She gave the address and wished him good-bye.

Mrs Trefusis was one of those ladies who spent the late afternoons in giving or attending tea-parties, not from love of the beverage, but for the opportunity it gave of displaying cherished articles of clothing and, it must be confessed, of exchanging confidences about neighbours. On this day it was not surprising that she had chosen to be hostess, for there was the funeral of the murdered woman to be discussed together with the identity of the murderer. The maid who answered the doorbell took Richardson's card by the corner and looked doubtful.

"There's a lot of ladies here, sir. Do you wish to see the mistress alone?"

"If you please."

When the drawing room was opened there was a clatter of feminine tongues. In the hush that followed the presentation of his card he heard a hoarse whisper. "It's the big detective man from Scotland Yard."

"Have him in here," exclaimed a jocular voice.

"No, I'll have to go out to him."

"I've been wondering when one of you gentlemen would call upon me," was her greeting to Richardson in the hall. "Up till now I've had no one but the reporters. Come into the dining room: we shall be quite to ourselves there."

She motioned him to a chair and sat down, prepared to enjoy herself.

"I've called to ask you a very simple question, Mrs Trefusis. You will remember that on the night before the murder of Mrs Pomeroy you were present at a bridge party attended by Mr and Mrs Pomeroy."

"Am I ever likely to forget that party?"

"Well, this is a small detail, but I hope that you will remember it. Were cigars provided for the guests?"

"Good gracious! What a question! Yes, and very good cigars too; so my husband said, and he's a good judge."

"Can you remember whether all the four gentlemen smoked a cigar?"

"Oh yes. They were the best Havana cigars, so my husband told me."

"And Mr Pomeroy accepted one with the rest?"

"Yes. Why, is that cigar a clue against him?" she added with her eyes glistening. "You know, last night we were discussing whether my husband and Mr Claremont should go to the funeral, and we decided against it, because one doesn't like to be mixed up in affairs like this and with all this suspicion against Mr Pomeroy. You see, people forget all the details; all that sticks in their memory is that you were mixed up in a murder case, and that isn't very nice, is it?"

"But Mr Pomeroy has been released."

"Yes, and I ask myself why, when the evidence was so strong against him. You know, I can talk to you confidentially as you're a police officer. That woman deliberately stole Mrs Meadows' ring that night when the lights went out, and of course Mr Pomeroy knew she had. It wasn't the first time by many that he had had to suffer from her kleptomania."

"Thank you, Mrs Trefusis. I don't think I need detain you any longer."

"Stop! I hear my husband's latchkey. Jack, come in here a moment." A burly Englishman blocked the door. "Come in and shut the door behind you. This gentleman is from Scotland Yard. He wants to know whether all of you men accepted a cigar when we played bridge at the Claremonts' that night."

"Yes, I think so—all four of us. But to make sure we'll ring up Claremont."

Richardson tried to interpose, but the number had already been called, and he listened to the conversation. "I know I took one and jolly good it was, but what about Pomeroy? You're sure he took one?...He was smoking it when he left the house? Thanks, old man, that's all we wanted to know." He rang off.

"Claremont says yes."

"Thank you," said Richardson. "I only wanted to make sure."

"You'll let us know if it turns out to be very important, won't you?"

Richardson laughed. "I'm afraid, Mrs Trefusis, that it is only a very minor point, but in cases like this, one cannot afford to neglect anything. Good-bye."

Mrs Trefusis' last endeavour to detain him took a despairing form. "If you encounter any other difficult point you won't fail to come and consult us, will you?"

But Richardson appeared to be afflicted with sudden deafness and merely waved his hand.

Although this might have been held to bear against the theory that the cigar had been dropped by a stranger, Richardson did not allow himself to be depressed until he had carried the investigation further. He returned to the police station and asked Aitkin whether he had still in his possession the key of the bungalow.

"Yes, fortunately I have. I took it to the father's house, meaning to give it up to Pomeroy, but he was ill in bed, so I kept it until he should come to ask for it." He unlocked his desk and produced a key. "Would you like me to come to the bungalow with you?"

"Yes. I'll tell you why when we get there."

"Hammett and I have been having a day of it. You'd think that half the population of this suburb had been in the neighbourhood of that bungalow from before daylight on the morning of the murder, and that the other half had been walking round it stealthily all night. All these informants could swear to having seen prowlers about."

"That always happens."

"I know, but think of the time it wastes."

"Yes, but think of what one might lose if you shooed them all away without listening to them."

"These informants didn't come forward at all until they heard what we were in search of. Our first quiet enquiries in that direction drew blank, and, after all, we ought to be glad that people are so ready to help us out of our difficulties."

Each visit to that bungalow seemed more depressing than the last, but Richardson did not allow himself to be unduly depressed. He explained the object of their visit in the fewest words.

"I want you to hunt through the building for the stub of a cigar. My own impression is that what we ought to find is a short stub. You see, a stub was picked up by one of those visitors to the bungalow just under the outside doorstep, and I have just learned that Pomeroy smoked a cigar on the way home on the night before the murder."

"Well, why look for the stub indoors if it was picked up outside the building?"

"Because if a stub was picked up inside as well as outside it would prove that some stranger had come to the house late that night or in the early morning."

Thinking inwardly that he was about to waste his time on a fruitless search, Aitkin took off his coat and set to work.

"If we don't find one it won't be conclusive," observed Richardson almost to himself, "because cigar stubs smell, and cigar smokers often throw their stubs down the drain."

He had hardly finished speaking when Aitkin returned carrying an ash tray which he had found in Pomeroy's dressing room. In this was found the shortest cigar stub that Richardson had ever seen.

Chapter Ten

As Ann Pomeroy walked back from the funeral she was pondering in her mind why Richardson should have wanted Mrs Trefusis' address, and she arrived at a conclusion. The famous detective from Scotland Yard hoped to strengthen the evidence against her cousin Miles that he had left the bridge party strongly incensed against his wife over the episode of the ring. She knew enough of Mrs Trefusis to be sure that any story from her would lose nothing in the telling. The minds of the big men at Scotland Yard worked strangely. They had those letters written by Casey, they had the knowledge that he was in the habit of calling at the bungalow at the actual hour at which the murder must have been committed, and yet they seemed to have taken no action but to have swallowed whole the story that he told them to prove his alibi.

She heard her name called in a child's voice behind her and stopped. Pat Coxon ran up breathless.

"I saw you at the funeral, Miss Ann, and then suddenly I missed you and they told me that you had left the cemetery so I ran all the way after you, because I've something to show you."

He dived his hand into his trouser pocket and dragged out a handful of the conglomeration that is to be found in the pockets of schoolboys, lightly cemented together with melted toffee. From this he extracted a coin.

"Do you know what this is, Miss Ann?"

"It looks like a foreign coin."

"It isn't foreign, it's Irish."

"How do you know that it's Irish?"

"Because Mr Casey showed me one. And where do you think I found this?" he asked, lowering his voice significantly. "I found it in the brambles outside the Pomeroys' bungalow when I was looking for clues."

"Well, you are a clever detective, Pat. I hunted thoroughly and found nothing, and so did the police."

Pat's face assumed a look of serious importance. "I've decided to become a detective when I'm grown up," he said; "but don't be afraid. I'll go on with my drawing in my spare time."

"You may find it very useful to be able to draw in your detective work. Leave the shilling with me for the moment, Pat, and then we'll go together to the big man from Scotland Yard and tell him where you found it."

"I know him. He gave us some toffee one day and asked us a lot about Mr Casey. I think he has suspicions against him, like us, Miss Ann."

"I'll let you know when we can go to see him. This find of yours may prove to be very useful. In the meantime don't tell anyone about it. I won't ask you in now, but I promise that you shall go with me as soon as I can get Mr Richardson to see us."

Pat raced off, well pleased with the prospect of becoming, perhaps, an important witness in a case that was reported with illustrations in the newspapers.

Now that the funeral was over Ann felt a great relief from strain and was able to devote herself to neglected work for an hour or two. True to her promise to Pat that he should be present when she had her interview with Superintendent Richardson, she rang up the police station to know at what hour she could see him on the following morning, which happened to be a Saturday, when Pat would not be at school.

"The superintendent is here now, miss," was the answer. "Perhaps you would like to speak to him yourself. Hold on, and I'll put you through."

The conversation was a short one. "I have something here that I think you ought to see, Mr Richardson. I am Ann Pomeroy. Shall I come up to the police station with it tomorrow morning, and at what hour?"

"Not at all; I will come down to see you at your home at about ten o'clock."

"Thank you very much."

There remained now only to make sure that Pat should be there. She knew that there was a telephone in the Coxons' house, but it belonged to Mr Casey, and with an ironical smile she called the number. A voice with a Dublin accent replied, and adopting her most mellifluous tone she declared her identity and asked the speaker to give a message to the boy Pat, telling him to call upon her at a quarter to ten the following morning.

She had just determined to close down for the night and go to bed early when her own telephone rang.

"Arthur Grant speaking," said a voice.

"Arthur Grant?"

"Yes, you remember: the brother of the dead Mrs Pomeroy. I was at your house today."

"Of course. How stupid of me. For the moment I had forgotten the name."

"I promised to find out if I could the whereabouts of that actor fellow who might have been sponging on Stella."

"Yes. Have you got his address?"

"Listen. Will you let me give you some advice? I'm giving it to you in good faith. It is that you should let the whole matter drop. Believe me, it is far the wisest course. These things always die down and get forgotten in a day or two if you let them, but if one starts stirring them up again one never knows where they will end."

"But I particularly want to trace that coat, and you promised to help me."

There was a slight pause at the other end of the wire. Then the voice continued: "I am convinced that I can help you most by advising you to drop the whole matter."

"Thank you," said Ann shortly and rang off.

Here, at any rate, she reflected, is something that is likely to be of interest to Superintendent Richardson. She sat down and wrote out the conversation from memory, reflecting that when a doubtful kind of person urges a particular course there is something behind it.

On the following morning Pat Coxon was at the house punctually; there was a quarter of an hour to wait. Ann explained to him that as soon as he had shown his Irish shilling to the superintendent and explained where he had found it he must go, because she had other things to tell him.

"Couldn't I stay and protect you?" asked the boy earnestly. "I might be a great help to you."

"No, Pat, I'm afraid you must go. You see, before the superintendent allowed me to tell him anything he would open the front door and put you out, and if you resisted they might give you three months for obstructing the police in the execution of their duty."

There was no time for further protest: the front-door bell rang. "You may answer the door," said Ann, "and if it's Mr Richardson show him straight in here. Then we'll tell him all about the shilling and you will slip away."

Richardson listened with grave attention to Pat's story and examined the shilling.

"I stuck a stick in the exact place where the shilling was lying. You'll find it there now."

"If you go on like this you'll make a wonderful detective, young man, when the times comes. I suppose you'll like to keep this shilling as a memento of your first detective case. I shall go down later in the day and look for your stick. I shall also be putting you to an important test. If detectives are to be any use at all, they must first satisfy their superior officers that they can keep secrets. Mind, not a word of this to anyone, either boys or grownups. Treat it all as something that you have forgotten when you get out of this room."

Pat made a grave salute and left the room holding his head high.

"Now, Mr Richardson," said Ann when they were alone, "don't you think that this bears out my theory that Casey was mixed up in this affair?"

"Granted that the Irish shilling may have belonged to him, isn't it more likely that when he dropped it he was doing what we all have been doing—looking for some clue in the waste ground behind the bungalow? I went very carefully over that ground, and the shilling was not there when I looked."

"I suppose that you, like Mr Aitkin, think that that bloodstained coat belonged to my cousin."

"On the contrary, some enquiries that I have been making have established the ownership of that coat. As you know, a public road much frequented by motor vehicles runs a little over two hundred yards from the back of the bungalow. There was a serious motor accident there early in the month—a collision between a car and a motorcycle. The man on the motorcycle was badly injured and was taken to the hospital; the car owner offered to break the news to his wife and was taking that coat with him to her house. Then he reflected that to bring back a coat in that state would add very much to her alarm, and he rolled it up and concealed it in the undergrowth by the roadside, intending to let her know later where it would be found. This he neglected to do, but he came forward yesterday to tell the police as soon as he read about the coat in the newspapers."

Ann listened attentively. "Then the police have no evidence whatever against my cousin."

"That is so." Then he added with a smile, "Neither have they any evidence against Mr Casey."

"Well, this makes it more mysterious than ever. I have kept for you the notes of a conversation I had on the telephone with that man Grant yesterday. He had promised to help me to find the man to whom his sister, my cousin's wife, might have given the coat. This is a verbatim account of what passed."

Richardson frowned over the manuscript. "May I keep this?" he asked.

"Certainly. I wrote it out for you, but can you suggest any motive for all this mystery?"

"Mr Maddox took Mr Grant off to his hotel after the funeral, didn't he?"

"Yes, and promised to look after him. He may have the idea of giving Stella Pomeroy's share of that estate in New Zealand to her brother instead of to her husband, but I'm sure my cousin wouldn't care to take it."

"That, of course, is a question for the lawyers, not for me. Grant was to have given you the names of actors who might have been sponging on the dead woman. He didn't give you these?"

"Yes, he gave me two names but no addresses. I made a note of the names at the time. Here they are."

"Clement Wickham and Arthur Rowton," said Richardson, searching his memory. "No, they have not been before me in any case that I remember, but if I can use your telephone..."

"Whitehall 1212," demanded Richardson. "C.R.O. Index, please. Superintendent Richardson speaking. Have you any record against Clement Wickham or Arthur Rowton?...Nothing against Arthur Rowton. Clement Wickham once cautioned for sending begging letters. Thank you." He rang off and turned to Ann. "The information you have given me may turn out to be useful, Miss Pomeroy. At any rate you need not worry any more about that raincoat."

"I'm afraid I shall still have to worry until the real murderer is found, because there are people who look awkward when my cousin's name is mentioned. I have to clear him entirely—or rather, I ought to say that you have to."

"You can rely upon me doing my best." He stowed away in an inner pocket the notes that she had given him and took his leave. His next visit was to Divisional Detective Inspector Aitkin at the police station. He found him wading through a sheaf of papers, dividing them into two heaps. This separating of the grain from the chaff is a familiar practice whenever the public begins to take an interest in a crime, for every well-meaning person anxious to help in bringing a criminal to justice hastens to send in to the police what he believes to be useful information.

"Have you found anything useful among all those papers?"

"One or two that might be useful if they could be relied upon," replied Aitkin; "but I haven't yet found one that calls for action. In the whole of this lot there are no two which corroborate one another. The two nearest give descriptions of a stranger seen about nine o'clock near the bungalow, but their descriptions do not coincide. Here's one of them, from Mrs Banning, who occupies the last house before you come to the bungalow. She describes the man she saw as being under middle height and wearing a dark-blue suit. She says that he walked up and down in front of her windows for some minutes; that she did not see what became of him because she had to get the breakfast. Mrs Wilson, who lives in the same road, also saw a man in a dark-blue suit, but he was a very tall man. She too failed to see what became of him."

"Alas, what a number of involuntary liars there are among us. How did these two people strike you?"

"They both thought that they were telling the truth."

"And when we see the man he will turn out to have been dressed in grey and neither short nor tall."

"The only point on which their evidence coincides is the time—nearly nine o'clock."

"Yes, because that was the hour for getting the children off to school. The longer I live the less confidence I put in the descriptions furnished by eyewitnesses."

"The others consist of people who say that they saw a tramp hanging about. One describes him as persistently begging for a cigarette and refusing to take No for an answer."

"Of course we can dismiss that kind of story. No tramp who killed a woman would have thought of putting her into a bath to make it appear that the death had been an accident. I shall probably be in London making enquiries for the next few days. You can always ring me up if any promising information comes your way, otherwise please continue to make a note of circumstances that seem to require attention. Of one thing we can be pretty sure—that some stranger did approach the front door that morning and drop a more than half-smoked cigar on the doorstep, which might signify that he intended to seek admission and was too polite to enter smoking, or that he found a cigar too strong for him."

Chapter Eleven

RICHARDSON'S first destination on reaching Paddington was the Palace Hotel. He wanted to catch Arthur Grant and Ted Maddox before they sallied forth for the afternoon. As he hoped, he found them in the bar with a third man, whom he guessed to be Otway, the fellow traveller of Maddox and the person of doubtful antecedents in New Zealand. The three men affected not to see him, which meant that he could not count upon a cordial welcome, for Grant and Maddox were obviously engaged in apprising their companion of the identity of the newcomer, much to the entertainment of the barman, who knew Richardson well and was always ready to help him.

"You're the very man I wanted to see," said Richardson to Grant. "I've something to tell you that you will be glad to hear. I suppose that I may talk freely here."

"Of course," said Maddox, joining in and shaking hands. "We are all friends here. Ah, I forgot; you do not know my friend Mr Otway—he's from New Zealand like myself."

"Glad to meet you, Mr Otway."

"Well now, Mr Richardson, you'll have something?"

"I never drink in the morning."

"Oh come, a sherry won't hurt you. Bring a sherry over to this table, John," said Maddox to the barman, and led the way to a table at some little distance from the bar.

"Well," said Richardson as they sat down, "I came to relieve Mr Grant's mind about his brother-in-law, Miles Pomeroy. You will be glad to know that the mystery about that bloodstained coat has now been cleared up. It did not belong to Mr Pomeroy."

"Have you found another suspected person?" asked Maddox before Grant could reply.

"No, the coat had nothing whatever to do with the case." He related the true story of the coat and then turned to Grant. "I know you were worried about your brother-in-law's missing raincoat. You had promised to help Miss Pomeroy to trace it."

Grant's alert look of suspicion was not lost upon Richardson, neither was the furtive look of enquiry which he threw at Maddox as if he was to be the prompter in the piece.

"Oh," he said, "I don't know that I exactly promised to help her."

"She thinks you did. You were to find the person to whom that raincoat may have been given, and last night you rang her up and told her that she had better drop the whole thing. Why was that?"

Again Grant looked at his prompter, who came to his rescue.

"Well, as a matter of fact, Mr Richardson, we had been talking the case over between us, and we came to the conclusion that it was no good beating about the bush; that everything pointed to Pomeroy as having been the guilty person, and that his cousin would be only burning her fingers if she pushed her enquiries any further. That is why Grant rang her up."

Otway broke in for the first time. "I daresay that I was partly responsible for this. I warned them that they might get an innocent actor drawn in, as happened in a case I heard of some years ago."

It was a moment for Richardson to dissemble—to let it appear that he, too, could be an innocent dupe. "Oh, I understand now," he said, rising to go. "Clouds seem to be thickening about Pomeroy—poor wretch."

He took particular note of the demeanour of the men as he shook hands—of the manifest relief of Grant, of the assumed joviality of Maddox, of the well-acted indifference of Otway—for in dealing with his criminal acquaintances Richardson never neglected to relieve their minds during the parting handshake.

His next quest was in the office of the steamboat company, in the hope of encountering either the purser or some other officer of the *Aorangi* of the New Zealand line. There he learned that the *Aorangi* was sailing next day and if he wished to see any of the officers he should seek them on board the steamer at the docks.

As he came out into the street he ran into Maddox, who, to do him justice for histrionic talent, appeared astonished at the encounter.

"Are you going on a foreign trip, Mr Richardson? You didn't tell us that half an hour ago."

"In my job one never knows from minute to minute where one may be sent," retorted Richardson. He knew that Maddox had been employed in shadowing him, and he carried the war into the enemy's camp. "And you, Mr Maddox? Are you booking a passage too? Have you got tired of England already?"

"Unfortunately they're so slow in England over probate business I don't know when I shall get this will proved, and until I do I shall have to stay here. But all the same I like to keep myself informed about the sailings."

"Ah, I see—as a cure for homesickness." He hailed a passing taxi and called to the driver, "To Scotland Yard." As soon as a glance through the little window at the back assured him that his taxi was not being shadowed, he tapped on the glass behind the driver and changed his destination to the West India dock. There he was fortunate enough to find the purser on board. From him he learned that the bedroom steward of these two young men could be seen. This steward had a perfect recollection of the two and remembered to which of the dock porters he had given their hand luggage. He was able to call up the man, who told him that when he offered to carry the luggage to a taxi, they had declined and desired him to put it in the cloakroom, where they would call for it later in the day.

"Did they take a taxi when they left the docks?"

"Yes sir, I believe they did. Leastways, I remember them asking me where the rank was."

This tracing of a particular taxi was a job for a junior officer, and he would confide it to one from the Central Office. He felt that the time had now come for him to take counsel with his chief.

He sent up his name to Morden and was admitted immediately.

"Well, Mr Richardson, I've been wondering how you were getting on. Your reports don't tell us very much."

"No sir, there hasn't been very much to tell so far. All that I can say positively is that the husband of Stella Pomeroy had nothing to do with her murder and was quite properly released."

"Well, that's something, but not very much. What about the lover whom you mentioned in one of your reports?"

"I think it is too early to dismiss him from the case, but Inspector Aitkin is keeping an eye upon him. I came to take instructions from you about three new individuals in the case, of whom two have turned up from New Zealand." He described the relationship between the dead woman, Grant and Maddox, and the terms of the will of the New Zealand sheep farmer.

"Would Maddox stand to benefit by the death of Stella Pomeroy?"

"No sir; that is where any motive fails us. The only person to benefit will probably turn out to be the husband of the dead woman, Miles Pomeroy."

"Then what have you against Maddox?"

"To tell you the truth, sir, I have nothing against him except my own personal suspicion."

"Was he in the neighbourhood that morning?"

"He arrived, apparently for the first time, at the bungalow during the confusion following the discovery of the body; but I have ascertained this morning that his steamer tied up in the West India dock in time to allow him to arrive at the bungalow in Ealing at the hour when the murder was committed, and that he left his luggage in the cloakroom and went off from the docks in a taxi."

"If that's all you've got to go upon I don't envy you the job of proving your case against him. You haven't forgotten, of course, that a stranger arriving from New Zealand and in London for the first time in his life would know nothing about railways or underground, and would take a taxi the whole way. He would know that Ealing was in the London area. It is curious that no taxi driver reading of the murder has come forward to say that he drove a stranger from the docks to the Ealing village settlement that morning; they are generally so ready to come forward with information."

"I know sir, and I'm putting P.C. Dunstan onto that very enquiry. He is, as you know, in the Public Carriage Department. As regards the local enquiries, they have been covered by the D.D.I."

"Inspector Aitkin?"

"Yes sir."

"Have you cured him of his obsession that the husband was the murderer?"

"I think so, sir, though it wouldn't take much to put him back into that error again."

"You say that you think Otway may have had a criminal career in New Zealand. We ought to be able to verify that by cabling in cipher to Wellington."

"Yes sir. If you will authorize this I will see to it. In the meantime I should like to put those three men in the Palace Hotel under discreet observation."

"I'm not a believer in observation of obvious crooks. They always tumble to it. Probably this man Otway is a past master in the art of shaking off followers, and at this point it seems to me you ought not to risk alarming them."

"Perhaps you are right, sir. I believe that Maddox is already on the alert and was following me this morning: that's why I have to be very careful."

"You could probably make some quiet arrangement with one of the hotel servants without incorporating it in your report."

"I have one hope, sir. The man Grant is a weak-kneed fellow who might come out with everything he knows if he's properly handled, but I'm not sure that he knows enough yet to be of use to us."

"Well then, when the moment comes you might try the pressure of putting him under clumsy observation —the kind of observation that he could not help noticing. You might convert him into becoming a useful informant."

Richardson nodded. He knew from experience in other cases that the one thing which the criminal afflicted with nerves cannot withstand is the knowledge that he is being followed wherever he goes.

"Very good, sir. I may have to draw upon an informant who is known to yourself."

"You mean Mr Milsom. Do so if you think it necessary, but don't refer to it, of course, in any of your reports. Now we had better send that cipher cable to New Zealand."

He took up a cable form. "We'll mark it 'priority' and get the people upstairs to cipher it. 'Police, Wellington. Cable any criminal record against Charles Otway. N.S.Y.' This will get through in the middle of the night when the man on duty in Wellington will be little better than a watchman. We can't count on getting a reply under five or six hours."

"No sir, but if I am not here I shall be down at Ealing. You could have the message telephoned to me there."

Richardson took the message upstairs to be ciphered and then glanced at the clock. If his friend Jim Milsom were lunching at home, as sometimes happened, he would be in time to catch him. He made for the building of service flats and was in time to catch his friend as he was about to sit down to his meal.

"You are just in time," exclaimed the publisher, slapping him on the shoulder. "I was going to have a solitary meal. Now, in your agreeable company, I shall expand, eat a colossal meal and sleep it off in my office, unless; you let me cart you to some exciting adventure in the; car. Even my uncle could not find fault with that as a way of spending an afternoon."

"I did not come to sponge on you for luncheon. I came to ask whether you could help us by undertaking a little job of observation."

"Could I not? It's the one spring that my thirsty soul has been panting for—no disguise needed, just the silly old publisher chap who's always poking in his nose where he's not wanted. No one could suspect him of being a police nark. Come along in and let me feed you."

"On one condition, Mr Milsom: that we keep off shop until the waiters have left us. They all know me, and their ears will be flapping. We will talk about the weather and the League of Nations, if you don't mind."

When they had exhausted the political field and the waiters had left them to their coffee, Richardson said, "You remember our last talk about that Ealing case, when you told me that you centred your suspicions on Otway and asked me to watch him? Well, that's exactly what I'm now going to ask you to do."

"Steady. Maddox might remember me. We passed the time of day in the garden of the bungalow on that morning of the murder."

"Oh, you never told me that. This may mean a change in our plans. He is staying in the Palace Hotel with Otway and the murdered woman's brother, a man named Arthur Grant."

"How does the brother come into it?"

"Out of sheer weakness and impecuniosity, I fancy. Maddox met him at the funeral and took him away with him to his hotel."

"That's just what we don't know. Presumably it is to make a cat's-paw of him in some way. I had hoped that you would get me some useful information on that point."

"Well, then I suppose it will have to go, and I shall be left to mourn it with a horrible feeling that I have come out partially unclothed."

"What are you talking about?"

"My moustache, of course. What else?"

"Oh, that moustache may make all the difference in the world. When he saw you he was agitated and only half took you in, and although there isn't much of it beyond a smudge under each nostril, it may make all the difference. It's worth trying."

"So that's the cold-blooded way in which you accept my sacrifice in the interests of justice? I wonder that you get anybody to work for you. But go on, give me my orders."

"Now, I don't suggest that you should be victimized to the extent of taking a room at the Palace, but I don't think that it would be difficult for you to cultivate relations with them by finding your way to their hearts down their throats."

"You mean there is a bar at the Palace? And if I told you that in deference to my uncle I had joined the prohibitionists…?"

"I shouldn't believe you."

"Well, of course, in deference to you and in entire disregard for my own interests I'll take it on, but you must indicate the moment when my secret observation is to become apparent. When, for example, I am to whip out a pocket Kodak, spin round in front of the trio, snap them and make off at top speed."

"All that shall be done. But, seriously, it is essential that they should not guess that you and I are acquainted with one another. Maddox already thinks me worth keeping under observation."

"Right. I'll send you all the information I gather by post or by telephone."

"We have cabled to New Zealand asking for any criminal record against our friend Otway. You shall have the reply as soon as I get it. For the next day or two I shall be lying doggo down at Ealing to allay the suspicion of Maddox that I am deeper than I look."

"I can't for the life of me see why Maddox should have killed that woman when he had no chance of getting hold of her money. He must share the old man's fortune with her heir, and her heir is her husband. Anyone would have told him that. Even if he knew that he would have to share the fortune with her husband and hoped to get him removed by the hangman, there would still have been another heir."

"I think that the crime was unpremeditated—the result of a sudden quarrel. We've no means of knowing what the quarrel was about, but I have no doubt at all that it had to do with the division of the property in some way."

"Look here. To me the case seems quite simple. Mrs Pomeroy had passed her youth in New Zealand, hadn't she? Good. She had a passion for the stage, hadn't she? Good. That meant that she was larky, and larky young women in New Zealand, like everywhere else, have lovers. Well, there you are. Otway was her lover: it was what the French call a *crime passionnel*—a crime of passion."

"Otway doesn't strike me as a man who would commit a crime for passion—for filthy lucre if you like, but not for disappointed love."

"My dear Richardson. You distinguished police officers go about your work in blinkers. You know nothing of the ravages of the human heart as we do out in the world. Why, as a publisher of thrillers mostly written by passionate women, I have double your advantages. Disappointed love, my authoresses tell me, is the most fruitful source of murder that can be found anywhere. Let me send you a few books to prove it."

"It's very kind of you, but I won't trouble you to do that. We police officers are brought face to face with cases quite as poignant as any that you can find in the novels, and they have the advantage of being true."

"Well, Superintendent, I have my orders. This very evening I shall go and take my cocktail at the bar in the Palace Hotel, if I can arrange it, in the company of the travellers from New Zealand."

"Before I go there's one thing you might try to remember—Maddox's demeanour when he arrived at the bungalow. Was he agitated?"

"Well, now I come to think of it, he was. He was mopping his brow, breathing hard and quite unable to keep still. I thought that it was the surprise of the news of his cousin's death that had upset him, but it would fit in very well with the other thing. In plain English he was as nervous as a cat, but leave it to me: I'll watch him."

Chapter Twelve

THE BAR at the Palace Hotel seemed to have been especially designed by the architect for the business which Milsom had in hand. He had armed himself with a cable form and was apparently struggling with composition at one of the little tables when the two travellers from New Zealand drifted over to the bar for their evening refreshment. Milsom recognized Maddox at once. He allowed them a little rope before he, too, slouched over to the barman with a request for information.

"Supposing I send a cable to Wellington in New Zealand now, what time of day would they get it out there?"

This appeared to be a riddle which had never been put to the barman before. He suggested applying to the office for the information, but Maddox interposed.

"I can tell you that, sir. Seven o'clock in the evening here is about seven o'clock in the morning in Wellington. You ought to be able to count upon getting a reply to your cable first thing in the morning. It all depends upon the line being clear."

Milsom thanked him and begged the two to share a drink with him.

"You seem to know all about cabling to Wellington," he said when the drinks were served.

"We ought to. We started from Wellington just over five weeks ago."

"It's a very nice place, I believe."

"Oh, it's all right, but one soon gets through it. Give me London every time," said the shorter man, whom Milsom guessed to be Otway.

Maddox laughed. "My friend Otway is a town bird, you see. I belong to the big open spaces out there. You see, I have a sheep run, and that means sticking to the country whether one likes it or not."

Milsom knew his type: knew that if once set going he would brag about the sheep run until he had produced the impression that he owned half the Dominion; that if he wanted to ingratiate himself he could do it in no way better than by encouraging him to boast; so for the next half-hour he invited his tongue to wag. With every sentence the man uttered, Milsom's dislike of him grew, and, as he reflected, it would have been so easy with a word or two to reduce the man to pulp, but without any effort that could be seen he contrived to conceal his feelings. There was one palliative: it was clear that he had not been recognized.

"Well," he said at last, "I dropped in here to pass the time, never thinking that I should meet such interesting companions."

"We're staying here," said Maddox. "If you care to drop in tomorrow or any day at this hour, you'll generally find us here. My name's Maddox."

"And mine's Hudson—Jim Hudson." This was true as far as it went. James was his first name and Hudson his second—his surname had escaped his memory for the moment.

Jim Milsom was feeling a little uneasy about Otway's silence. The man had allowed his friend Maddox to do all the talking, but he did second the invitation with cordiality, though his steady gaze upon their new acquaintance had been a little disturbing. Milsom decided that he had disarmed criticism, but that Otway would always prove to be a more difficult proposition than his blustering friend.

"I shall certainly look in again," he said, "and I promise in advance that I shall not abuse your invitation by dropping in too often."

He was about to take his leave when a man crossed the floor towards them, saying to Maddox, "Hallo, Ted."

Maddox introduced him as "My cousin, Mr Grant," but Milsom did not stop to make his further acquaintance.

On reaching his own flat he went straight to the telephone and called up Richardson at Ealing Police Station.

"Is that you, Superintendent? This is your friend J.H.M. speaking. I want to give you my first impression of that trio. Make your mind easy: I wasn't recognized—I could swear to that."

"That's good. Now for your impressions."

"Well, the first violin was almost too vocal to be healthy. I got him going on the Antipodes, but when it came to personalities he was evasive. For example, the sheep run that he was boosting melted away when I asked him whether it belonged to him. In a way it did, but when pressed for details it didn't. The subject was changed without any definite answer to that question."

"I shouldn't alarm him by asking any personal questions at first."

"You can trust me for that. When he invited me to call again I said that I should be delighted; that I had feared that he was only staying the night at the hotel and that we might not meet again. He said, 'If I could get a move on in this worn-out old country you wouldn't see my back for smoke, but these hidebound lawyers in England are the limit, and if I am to get my business settled I've got to stick on here and wait their good pleasure.' The other chap, Otway, seems to be quite content with London and not at all in a hurry to get back to the Antipodes."

"Did you see Grant?"

"Yes. He was a nervous sort of chap with 'poor relation' written all over him. What beats me is why Maddox should be footing the bill for those other two fellows, because he struck me as rather a mean bloke."

"Unless the other two hold the whip hand over him in some way."

"Exactly. Don't think that I want to chuck the job just at the moment when I am becoming the white-haired boy. I shall have them eating out of my hand before I've done with them."

"Well, I have a reply to my cable asking for O's record. It will be useful to you to know exactly what it is. He has had three pre cons—you know what pre cons means?"

"My agile brain has grasped the point. Three pre cons. You can go on."

"Three pre cons for gambling offences. Keep him away from cards and you may bring his life to an untimely end. He can't live without them. So don't be tempted to join him in a little flutter. You promised your dead mother never to touch a card if he should ask you to play with him. Apart from that little weakness they don't seem to have much against him out there."

"I'll remember your warning, but I may be tempted, nevertheless, if only to see how it's done."

"Well, be careful. And now I must ring off."

Jim Milsom was feeling so happy about his success as a sleuth that he had forgotten all about the loss of his moustache and was eager to see his adventure through. During the next day he found himself rehearsing his part for the evening. Like his new acquaintance, Otway, he too would be a devotee of the gambling table, but being a stranger to London he could not act as a guide.

The hour of half-past six found him once more in the bar of the Palace Hotel, and a few minutes later he was joined by the two New Zealanders. There was no air of distrust about them. They swallowed down their aperitif with relish, and then the talk turned quite naturally to cards.

"In this old town of London, one can't get what one would call a game. One can sit down to a game of bridge, of course, but the points are so low that they are not worth playing."

"Pardon me," said Otway in a low voice. "I haven't been wasting my time. I can take you to a place a short walk from here where we can join in a game that's worth playing."

"Where's that?"

"Close to Piccadilly Circus—a nice little upper room, and if by bad luck the flicks break in we are just a respectable little debating society, drinking lemonade and discussing the British policy in the Mediterranean."

"I suppose it's too early to go now?"

"Not at all. We can dine downstairs—the cooking is quite decent—and then a flight of stairs brings you into the room where business is done. In fact it's a better plan to go there early, because there's less danger of a raid: the flics make their raids as late as possible because then they have two strings to their bow— gambling and selling liquor after hours."

"They may know you there, but probably they'd stop me at the door and not let me in."

"Not if I introduce you as a pal of mine—one who likes a flutter and doesn't mind losing a bit now and then. Of course you're not bound to lose. A pal I took in there the other day came away with his pockets stuffed and all won in the last fifteen minutes he was there."

"Very well then. You shall be my guests at dinner. We'll do ourselves well, and then we'll get to business and we'll do ourselves better still. What about it?"

If Milsom had been in any doubt about his identity being suspected it was immediately dispelled. The two New Zealanders accepted his invitation with alacrity, and, it being now about the time for dinner, they moved off to an unpretentious little restaurant in a side street off Shaftesbury Avenue. Here there seemed to be an understanding between the head waiter and Milsom's guests: they were given a choice of tables, and they chose one close to the staircase. Milsom consulted his guests about their fare and the drinks of their preference, and he ordered them what he considered a very generous meal. Then came the moment when Otway suggested a visit to the room upstairs. Here they found themselves in an overcrowded room in a stifling atmosphere, the windows shut and curtained, with a table of some size almost hidden by the people of both sexes crowding round it. A game was in progress. The visitors were so thick about it that it was impossible to see what the game was, but Milsom, with his superior stature, caught a glimpse of a little rat-faced man manipulating a pack of cards and of people handing notes and silver to be staked on the table if their arms were not long enough to reach the green cloth themselves. A croupier with a rake was at work pushing winnings to some gamblers and raking in the contributions of the losers. Milsom speculated on what would happen if a raid took place; what evidence the raiders would be able to produce in court when there might be twenty witnesses to swear that it was a meeting of the Young Men's Christian Association. He decided that without a witness produced from inside the room the police would have difficulty in proving their case. The waiter who had passed them up the staircase would be equally capable of sounding an alarm.

There was no difficulty in evading the observation of Otway, the gambler, who seemed to scent the game before he had actually entered the room. With the dexterity of the habitual he had insinuated his body through the crowd until he had found a place at the table. His companion, Maddox, slithered in behind him, leaving their host, Milsom, in a good place for observing them.

Just as Otway reached the table Milsom observed a man who was sitting farther down the room trying in vain to catch his eye. Before Otway had time to seat himself the man rose and came face to face with him. They did not speak, but Milsom detected a significant glance pass between them, and Otway inclined his head in the direction of Maddox. Then the man returned to his seat and Otway sat down.

Whether the game was played fairly or not was not the question; the point was that it was a game and that some of the players won or were allowed to win. One thing was obvious: that Maddox was compelled to supply his companion with funds to continue the game when he lost and that this was happening oftener than suited the feelings of the almoner. It was a point to be noted and to be reported in due course to Richardson.

Nearly an hour passed before Milsom changed his place and took up a position behind the banker, partly in order to keep a watch on his proceedings and partly to be in a position to catch the eye of his guests. As regards the banker nothing to his detriment could be said: he appeared to be conducting the game quite fairly, the bias being always in favour of the bank. Presently Milsom chanced to catch the eye of Maddox, who must have been as tired of supplying his gambler-friend with funds as he himself was of watching the two. A moment later his arm was touched: Maddox had left his place and had come round to the other side of the table.

"You're not playing?"

"No, I thought I would wait until my next visit. I wanted to get the hang of the game first. How have you two been doing?"

"Only so-so; but it's hopeless to try and get Otway away until the luck turns solid against him. Up to now he's been keeping more or less level, but I've moved away purposely, because as long as he thinks that he can count upon a banker at his elbow nothing will stir him."

"He's lucky in having a banker; the other losers can't count on one."

"No, and the sooner he learns that there is an end to good nature, the better. I'm not going to finance him forever: I can't do it. It's the very devil to get these English lawyers to do what they're paid for doing. I want to get quit of this country and get back. Otherwise the whole of that sheep run of mine will be going to the devil, and with that gambling spirit of his, Otway will be broke to the wide. Ah, look at that. See the croupier's rake? That's been a nasty jar. All he's won and all I've lent him gone in one swoop. He'll be ready to come now."

Otway was looking wildly round for help, and finding no finance minister at his elbow he got up and slithered his way through the crowd to the outer circle of spectators. His two friends joined him, and without a word he led the way down the stairs, where the waiter wished them a cordial good night and assured them that they would be welcome on the morrow. There was no conversation between the three on the way home. Milsom wished them good night at the door of the Palace Hotel, saying to Otway, "Next time we go I want you to initiate me into the noble game."

"I will," said Otway eagerly. "You shall come and sit down just beside me, and we can make our stakes together."

Arrived at his own flat Jim Milsom rang up Richardson and recounted his doings of the evening.

"One thing I noticed may suggest something to you," he said. "In moments of emotion, that is to say when the wrong card turned up, I noticed that Maddox tugged at a moustache that wasn't there. In my own naked case I could feel for him, but it will require your perspicacity to explain why the expected moustache was not in its place. In my case, of course, I had the histrionic excuse that I am playing a part, but what excuse has he got? Who is out to recognize him?"

"H'm! It'll pay me to devote a little thought to the answer to that question. You say that he had to foot Otway's losses at the gambling table and that he did it with a bad grace—and yet he did it."

"Yes. It seemed obvious to me that Otway has some hold over him."

"What about Grant? Did you see him?"

"No, I'm afraid I've been neglecting Grant."

"He's worth cultivating, because I take him to be made of the weak stuff that can't keep a secret."

"I shall attend to the gentleman tomorrow. Meanwhile that gambling hell is on my mind. I don't say that it's doing any particular harm to the body politic, but you fellows at the Yard will never have such a chance again. An observer inside the room who can sound a peculiar whistle; a furniture van stuffed with police constables in and out of uniform with nothing to do but dash upstairs. What more can you want for a first-class raid, with me sprawling over the table to protect the notes and silver?"

"Thank you very much, but if you have a fault it is that your imagination is apt to run away with you. When it comes to raiding gambling hells I shall be glad to give you a first-class recommendation to the proper officer and you will cover yourself with glory. At the moment you and I are engaged in hunting higher game."

Chapter Thirteen

MILSOM'S telephone conversation had given Richardson ample food for thought. As Mr Morden had suggested, if Maddox was to have reached Ealing by nine o'clock on the morning of the murder he must have taken either a taxi from the docks, a private car from a neighbouring garage, or a train to Ealing and a taxi from Ealing station. The enquiries of the police constable Dunstan of the Public Carriage Department at the Yard had negatived all three alternatives, and yet how else could Maddox have accomplished the journey? It was true that he behaved as if he had something to hide; Milsom had already confirmed his suspicion that he was for some reason in Otway's power. Supposing that Otway knew that Maddox had been at the bungalow at nine o'clock that morning, he was far more likely to use that knowledge for purposes of blackmail than to come forward and denounce him to the police. As for Grant, he was perhaps weak enough to get into anybody's power, but he was not the type of man who would keep his mouth shut if he knew that a person with whom he was associating had murdered his own sister. No, decidedly, he had failed to find any evidence that would justify holding Maddox in this country if he wished to leave it.

It was borne in upon Richardson that he was not getting on.

At that moment the telephone rang. He supposed that it was a message for Inspector Aitkin, whose room he was using, but he took up the receiver and heard a woman's voice.

"Is that Superintendent Richardson?"

"It is."

"It's not Inspector Aitkin or any other officer speaking?"

"No. Who is speaking? It is Superintendent Richardson himself."

"Ann Pomeroy."

"I ought to have recognized your voice, Miss Pomeroy. What can I do for you?"

"I want you to come round to the bungalow as quickly as you can, and I want you to come alone. You'll find me waiting there for you. I'll bring the key with me."

"I'll start at once, but as I have a car here I will call for you at your house on the way."

He was not kept waiting. The front door opened as his car drew up. Ann Pomeroy had been on the lookout for him. She jumped in beside him and asked him to arrange with the driver to go slowly.

"I've a good deal to tell you while we're on our way to the bungalow. You know that Pat Coxon aspires to become a great detective. Well, he's been to me with a remarkable story. He's obsessed with the idea that Mr Casey was really guilty of the murder, and nothing will shake him of this belief. He told me that he was at choir practice this evening and that when he came out Mr Casey passed the boys going in the direction of the bungalow. He followed him at a discreet distance, meaning to keep him under observation, but when they got nearly to the bungalow Pat thought he would take a short cut and get there first. He reached the back of the bungalow just in time to see a man getting in through the scullery window, leaving it open. On this Pat followed the intruder in and stood listening. He heard the sound of drawers being pulled out in the bedroom and saw the reflection of a flash lamp. Unfortunately his little dog had also scrambled up through the window, and he began to bark when he found his master. The man extinguished his lamp, ran down the passage, knocked the boy over and escaped. It was too dark to make out who he was, but of course Pat is persuaded that it was Casey. He scrambled through the window after him, but it was too late, and he came straight to me to report what had happened."

"I must have an interview with this budding young detective. You know that at his age fancy plays a considerable part. I don't suggest that he was consciously lying, but one has to guard against unconscious exaggeration."

"I made an appointment for him to see me in the dinner hour tomorrow, and you could be present and question him as much as you like, but I thought that the quickest way of verifying his story would be for us both to go to the bungalow. We need not climb in through the scullery window, because I have the front-door key. If we find nothing disturbed, then you will have something to go upon when you question him." The car pulled up. Richardson led the way round to the back of the building to look at the scullery window. Thus far the story was borne out: an entry had been forced through that window, which was still ajar.

"Now, Miss Pomeroy, let us use your front-door key and see whether anyone has been in the bedroom." Richardson stood aside to allow Ann to precede him. She uttered a sharp exclamation when she entered. The boy's story seemed to be amply supported. Drawers had been pulled out and their contents scattered over the floor. A little apart from the wearing apparel of the dead woman lay three women's handbags, all gaping open. Silver coins and a few coppers were scattered on the floor near them and a powder puff or two. Ann was stooping to pick them up when Richardson intervened.

"Please don't touch them. Don't touch anything in the room. The driver of my car is quite competent to draw a plan, and he has a foot rule with him. I'll call him in."

He returned a moment later with the driver. "Huggins, I want you to make a rough plan of this room to scale. Be careful not to shift anything, and set out the exact position of those three handbags. While you're taking your measurements we'll get out of your way." To Ann Pomeroy he said, "We'll have a look round the other rooms and see whether anything has been stolen. Here's the dining room."

He pulled out a drawer in the sideboard and counted the spoons and forks. "No, the cutlery and plated ware appears to be intact—one dozen of each."

"It couldn't have been an ordinary burglar. The money out of the handbags in the other room was lying on the floor. The thief must have been after something else—letters, perhaps."

"Presuming the intruder to have been Mr Casey," said Richardson with a smile. "Well, now let's have a look at the marks in the scullery. It rained pretty heavily this afternoon, and you saw the mud outside the scullery window. What have we inside? Footprints. If you'll stand back I'll show you with my hand lamp. Here's a man's footprint, the boy's print is touching it, and the little dog has left his prints all over the place."

"That shows that Pat was speaking the truth, doesn't it?"

"Yes, it does, but I want you to look at the man's print. That's not the print of a man's outdoor shoe, it is the print of an evening shoe. The man who made it must have been wearing dress clothes. In that case we may find the prints of car wheels." While he was speaking he was taking the measurements of the footprint.

"Pat didn't mention a car; he would have told me if he had seen one standing near the bungalow."

"A car might easily have been parked on the other side of the bungalow without the boy noticing it. I'll go and look for wheel prints after you are gone. We'll go now and see whether Constable Huggins has finished his plan of the room, then he shall drive you home and come back for me. I'll bring the key of the bungalow to you tomorrow morning."

Ann hesitated as if she had something further to say. At last it came: "I suppose that you will take charge of those bags."

"Yes, the poor woman seemed to have a weakness for handbags."

Ann looked at him apprehensively. "Oh, it's no good having secrets from you, Mr Richardson. We are both thinking the same thing. You heard the evidence given at the inquest—about there having been a charge of shoplifting against Stella—a charge that came to nothing. Well, it's been a terrible worry to my cousin. You remember the evidence about that bridge party on the night before her death; every member of the party felt convinced that it was she who had secreted that ring when the lights went out. There are people who cannot resist the temptation to secrete pretty things."

"Yes, it is a form of mental weakness. We have instances of it every day. I see that Huggins has finished his plan. He shall take you home now, and I'll see you again in the morning."

Having conducted her to the car he went back to the bedroom and picked up the handbags, of which two appeared to be quite new. He then made a systematic search of the drawers and cupboards, and was rewarded by finding three more handbags and a parcel wrapped in tissue paper containing a bag bearing the initial E. Even Richardson's inexpert eye could judge that it was of high intrinsic value, and this was borne out by the hallmarks of the mountings. He decided to carry them all back to the police station with him and subject them to an intensive search. Before the return of the car he took out his hand lamp and made a careful search for car tracks outside the bungalow. Here there was no room for doubt. A car had been parked on the opposite side of the road, where it might easily have escaped the notice of an excited boy. Clearly some man in evening dress had come down by car and had broken into the bungalow to search for a lady's handbag. No one would have thought it worth while to take the risk of doing this unless the bag contained something of great value. What could the dead woman have had in her bag that was of sufficient value to tempt someone to break in? Had this any connection with the murder which he was investigating? The case was now taking on a new aspect.

As soon as Huggins returned with the car they went to the scullery window to make it secure against other intruders. Huggins' verdict after examining the fastening was, "The man who planned the security of this house was asking for trouble. No trained burglar would feel proud of getting into it. Look at this, Superintendent. Why, a child could slide back these bolts with a pocketknife. The wonder is that the place hasn't been broken into before. The burglars must have thought that there was nothing worth stealing."

"Yes, as you say, the men who fixed these catches on the window were asking for it. While you've been away I have discovered one thing—that the man who broke in was looking for something special. He may not have found it, and he may come back before morning for a second try. I suppose that you have screws and a screw driver in your tool kit?"

"Yes sir."

"Very well, then, we'll run a couple of two-inch screws diagonally into the window frame from inside: that'll stop them. Now help me to carry these bags to the car."

"Where to, sir?" asked Huggins as he took his seat at the wheel.

"Back to the police station."

Aitkin proved to be still in his office. Huggins followed his chief with an armful of ladies' handbags and spread them out on the table.

"You look as if you'd been robbing a bag shop, Mr Richardson," said Aitkin; "what's it going to lead to?"

"I can't promise to tell you that offhand, but it's going to lead somewhere. These bags all came from that bungalow."

"Why, the dead woman must have been a kleptomaniac."

"I think she was, but I think also that something more may come to light over this obsession of hers."

"A new clue to the murder, do you mean?"

"It might lead to that. We must take these bags and go through them. This evening a man broke into the bungalow, apparently in search of a particular bag or something that it contained." Richardson went on to describe what had happened. "These three bags were lying on the floor open. The money they had contained was scattered all over the carpet, which gave me the idea that it was a letter or paper of some kind that he was in search of. The other bags I found in the drawers. "Well go through them very carefully; even a visiting card in one of the pockets may help us."

"What I can't understand is why, when you were searching the bungalow with Hammett, you didn't notice the number of handbags in the woman's bedroom."

"We did notice them, but we put them down to feminine vanity."

The bags taken out of the drawers had every appearance of being new. Indeed, in one case there was a price ticket attached.

"This didn't cost nothing," said Aitkin, holding up the bag with the initial E; "but there's nothing in it."

Richardson took it from him and put it to his nose. "It's been used, though, and used by a lady who has a nice taste in scent. I suppose we could find the owner by advertising for her. As a matter of fact, we might describe all these bags in an advertisement and invite the owners to come forward. It might lead to something. Get one of your sergeants to draw up an advertisement for our police news, and we can get authority for inserting it elsewhere."

"Do you think the burglar found what he wanted?" asked Aitkin.

"I should think it doubtful whether he had time."

"Women are like magpies," observed Aitkin with reminiscence in his tone: "they hide things in funny places. I suggest that we go up to the bungalow tomorrow morning and search for a hiding place of a letter or paper, and as it was a woman who hid it we'll look in all the unlikeliest holes and corners."

"A woman who takes to living by her fingers, shoplifting, I mean, is sometime referred to as a kleptomaniac, as if she couldn't help it. No doubt she lacks some moral sense, but she knows perfectly well what she is doing and she trades upon her appearance as a protection against being found out. That was the case of this murdered woman, I have no doubt. From hints that

I had this evening from Miss Pomeroy, the husband knew her weakness and knew that it was growing upon her: that was why he was meditating a separation by getting himself transferred to a foreign branch of his bank."

"She may have had an accomplice," suggested Aitkin.

"She may, but we've got no trace of one yet. My idea is that the intruder this evening is in some way connected with the murderer."

"You discovered that the man who broke in this evening had come in a car. That would account for our difficulty in tracing a strange visitor on the morning of the murder. A private car might easily have left the main road and drawn up within reach of the bungalow without being seen by anybody."

"Yes. All the enquiries about taxis in the Public Carriage Office have drawn blank. But even a D.D. Inspector must sleep at times, and your night's rest is long overdue. I'll pick you up in the car at nine tomorrow morning, and well go down together to the bungalow."

On the drive home, Richardson did some hard thinking. Had he been wasting his own and his friend Milsom's time in chasing the wrong people? True, Otway had a reputation to hide, and clearly Maddox's manner was that of a doubtful personage, but one thing stood out—neither of these two men could have been the man who broke into the bungalow that evening, because they had a perfect alibi: they had been shepherding Jim Milsom to a gambling club. There remained only Grant to account for. Grant! The thought of that miserable weakling sent a shiver down his spine, for what could be more likely than that he should conceive the idea of crawling into an empty bungalow which had belonged to his dead sister in order to help himself to anything of value? At this thought the hope of a new clue, which had seemed so promising at first sight, began to fade. Richardson wisely resolved to dismiss the whole question from his mind until he should see what new light sunrise should bring on the morrow.

Chapter Fourteen

THE WEATHER favoured them next morning. The sun rose in a halo of autumn mist; the sky was cloudless. Richardson stopped the car a hundred yards short of the bungalow.

"Now, Mr Aitkin, I want you to look round. The murder took place on a morning very like this and at about the same hour. You and I get out of the car and make for the bungalow. Who would see us? There isn't a soul in sight. Who would even notice the car unless he were looking for it?"

"Schoolboys seeing a smart car would stop to have a look at it, but schoolboys don't come in this direction: they're to be found at the other end of the settlement."

"So that's one point established. A stranger could have arrived at the bungalow that morning without being seen. Now let us have a look at the wheel tracks of the car that came here last night. They've been drying pretty fast during the last couple of hours, but here they are clear enough. The man took his car off the road and parked it here in the soft ground, no doubt without lights. It was a biggish car—a twenty-horse to judge by the depth of the print in that soft ground at the roadside. And here's a point that might be useful for identification purposes. Here, where the car was backing off the road, we get the imprints of all four tires: the front tires are worn nearly smooth; there is a brand-new tire on the off side back wheel. Did you have a careful look at the car tracks on the morning of the murder?"

"It wasn't any good, Superintendent. By the time I arrived there were car marks all over the place—the people who had come to view the bungalow, to say nothing of the two doctors and a taxi."

"Yes, it would have been pretty hopeless to make any deductions that morning, but while we're inside the bungalow I'll get Huggins to have a careful look at those car tracks and see if they suggest anything. Before we go in let's have another look by daylight at the footprints outside the scullery window. Here we are. What do you make of them?"

"Well, these belong to the boy and these to the dog, of course. These others—h'm—I should say that they belonged to a man wearing a very light town shoe."

"Such as an evening shoe?"

"Yes sir."

"Well, when one passes to the other side of that window one finds exactly the same footprint on the tiles."

"Of course this window must have been very easy to break open: here are the marks of a penknife on the paintwork."

"Yes—before I got Huggins to screw it up on the inside. We might now go in and have a look at the bedroom. Here's the key of the front door."

The bedroom was exactly as it had been left on the previous night. Richardson slid back the curtains, letting in the sunlight. They stood for a moment in silence looking round the room.

"Well," asked Richardson, "what do you make of it?"

"I think it was a bag he was looking for, or rather, something contained in a bag. If it had been merely a document he would have gone first to the writing table and made a mess of the papers there, but, as you see, the desk is not locked and the papers are not disarranged."

"What could a lady carry in her handbag that would tempt a man to commit burglary to find it?"

"Well, if I may judge from my own wife, I should say that she carried everything in her handbag except the kitchen stove. Do you think it could have been drugs?"

"You mean that she was trading in drugs?"

"Why not? A woman who steals other women's bags, a shoplifter as this woman was, might descend to any kind of petty crime. At any rate I'm out to search this bungalow from rooftree to cellar. Drugs can be secreted in the smallest possible compass."

"They can, and the bungalow hasn't been searched as minutely as that. Go ahead, and good luck to you. I shall take the opportunity to call on Miss Ann Pomeroy and find out whether she has ever suspected her cousin's wife of being a secret drug taker."

On this occasion the little maid answered the bell and told Richardson that Miss Ann was upstairs in the sickroom. She was unwontedly communicative.

"You see, sir, Mr Pomeroy is going to get up this afternoon and he's got to go to his bank tomorrow morning, and that's why we're all so busy, but I'll call Miss Ann down if you like."

In view of the gravity of his question Richardson told her to tell Miss Ann that he would like to speak to her in her study. The little maid trotted upstairs with the message, leaving him standing in the hall Ann came down and took him into her den.

"I didn't expect you until midday. Pat won't be free until then."

"I came early because our search of the bungalow has raised a new and important question. Had you any suspicion, or has Mr Pomeroy ever hinted, that his wife took drugs?"

Ann looked shocked. "No, I never had that suspicion, and I'm sure that Miles would have told me if he suspected such a thing. Shall I go and ask him?"

"No, I shouldn't put the question point-blank like that."

"Oh, you needn't be afraid. He knows that you're here, and he'll want to know the reason for your early visit. I'll run up and ask him. He is so much better this morning that he talks of going to business tomorrow. I won't be more than two minutes."

The two minutes dragged on into five before a light step on the stairs announced her return.

"No, Mr Richardson. My cousin says that he has never suspected such a thing, and he doesn't think it possible that his wife could have been a drug addict without his knowledge."

"Is it possible, do you think, that she could have been trafficking in them without his knowledge?"

"I think that that's quite possible: she was alone in the bungalow all day long, and I know that she had visitors." She hesitated and then continued: "In view of all this I'm going to take you further into my confidence, Mr Richardson. Just recently Miles revealed to me that he was becoming alarmed at finding that Stella seemed to have some secret source of money, and he was terrified lest there should be some awful scandal of stealing money belonging to other people. I didn't mention it to him at the time, for fear of causing worse trouble between them, but I had a secret suspicion that she was accepting presents of money from Mr Casey."

"I think it would be a good thing if I were to see Mr Casey again, but of course I can't do it until the evening, when he comes home, and I am booked to have another interview with Pat at twelve o'clock. In the meantime I should like to ask whether it would be possible for me to have another look through that suitcase of letters belonging to the dead woman. Are they still here?"

"They are actually in this room. I'm sure that my cousin would like you to look through them again for anything you may want."

"I'm going to ask you to grant me a still greater favour— to allow me to go through them in this little room. I'm a tidy person: I shan't make any mess."

"Of course. I shan't be using the room before twelve o'clock. You can sweep all these papers off the table and spread out the letters. Here's the key of the case. I'll leave you to your task."

Richardson engaged in this new task with surprise that he had shirked it hitherto. He felt that somehow his old thoroughness was deserting him, that he was getting stale at his job—a sure sign that the curtain must be about to fall upon his efficiency as a detective as he had seen it fall upon so many of his colleagues. He remembered that when he last had these letters in his hands he had read but three of them, because he had ascertained, in the letter from Casey which he did read, that the man had been in the habit of calling at the bungalow each morning at the hour the murder was committed, and therefore it was probable that he had been there on that day. But on going into Casey's movements he had found that he had a satisfactory alibi for the thirteenth—that he had actually arrived at the office by an earlier train than usual. But that ought not to have absolved a detective of his experience from reading every letter, when he had the opportunity. Now was the moment for repairing the omission.

He read first the letters from the theatrical agencies; they were, of course, quite innocuous. Next the letters from the uncle in New Zealand: they proved no more than the fact, as he had discovered when he first read them, that they were calculated to arouse the dead woman's jealousy by their constant references to Ted Maddox in terms of affection and gratitude. But suddenly Richardson stiffened: one sentence had caught his attention:

What astonishes me is that a boy with such studious tastes as Ted should buckle to with work on a sheep farm—work, mind you, that is very fatiguing and leaves little time for reading. Yet Ted devours every book that he can lay his hands on.

A boy with such studious tastes; "Studious" was the last word that he would have thought of applying to young Maddox. If he was studious he was certainly giving his brain a rest while he was in England. He knew that Ann would excuse him if he used her telephone. He took up the receiver and called Jim Milsom at his publishing office.

"Is that you, Mr Milsom? Superintendent Richardson speaking. You have spent two evenings with Ted Maddox. Would you describe him as a young man of studious tastes?"

The reply was a guffaw reminiscent of a captive hyena at feeding time. "Who describes him as of studious tastes?"

"The man who adopted him as a son in New Zealand."

"Then someone has blundered."

"However that may be, I want you to bear this in mind when next you see him and study his character."

"I'll probe it to the bottom. As a publisher I ought to recognize a studious bloke when I see him. I shall start probing this very evening, beginning, of course, with Roger Bacon and finishing with P. G. Wodehouse."

"Do it seriously, because it may turn out to be a turning point in this case of ours."

"I see. Enter an impostor; the woman points a finger at him in denunciation; he lays her out with a hammer. See the *Daily Thrill*. But don't let my flippancy worry you. I'll do my job tonight as you would have it done. Good-bye."

Richardson returned to his chair and went meticulously through the remainder of the uncle's letters. They provided nothing more, and he turned to the bundle of Casey's letters. He had not read more than three before he understood Ann Pomeroy's comment that they made her sick. They were filled with greasy sentiment and poetical fantasy which went far from ringing true. He referred to her husband always as "the nuisance" or "the stumbling block." And then a passage caught his attention.

> We must always remember to be careful about the stumbling block. The game we are engaged upon is a very dangerous one.

The game! What game? The game of hide-and-seek of a guilty couple? Did he mean that? True, it would be a dangerous game for both of them, because Pomeroy was just the kind of man who might drag them into the divorce court, and such publicity wouldn't be good for Casey. On the other hand, in the light of his new suspicions, could the dangerous game be the selling of drugs? There must be no relaxation of the watch that must be kept on Casey. There could be no better position for acquiring a knowledge of where drugs could be obtained than that of a Fleet Street journalist. All this was pure conjecture, and Richardson felt that he must have far more evidence before he could venture to build upon this theory. He returned to his task of discovering other references to the "game," but nothing more incriminating than that which he had already found came to light.

The front-door bell rang. The little maid came into the hall from the back regions but was stopped on her way by Ann, who opened the door herself and ushered Pat into her little den. The boy swelled with importance when he found himself alone with Richardson.

"Good morning, young man. I've got a few questions to ask you, and I mustn't keep you, or your dinner will get cold. You told Miss Pomeroy about your adventure at the bungalow last night. What made you so certain that the man who climbed in through the scullery window was Mr Casey?"

"Well sir, you see I was shadowing Mr Casey at the time."

"Yes, but you took a shorter cut to the bungalow, and the man you saw getting in through the window had got there before you."

"Yes sir, he had."

"And last night it was dark: there was no moon. What could you have seen about him to distinguish him from other men?"

"I've been thinking over what happened, sir, and I think that I may have been wrong when I thought it was Mr Casey."

"Why?"

"Well sir, Mike, my dog, knows Mr Casey, and he wouldn't bark at him."

"But Mike may have been barking with joy at finding you in the bungalow."

"At first he did, but then he began growling and sniffing, and when the man came out of the bedroom he flew at him and barked in a different kind of way, like he does at strangers."

"Did you see a motorcar near the bungalow?"

"No sir, not a sign of one."

"Of course you didn't look round very much. All you thought of when you saw a man getting in through the scullery window was to follow him in."

"Yes sir, and if Mike hadn't barked I might have caught him in the act when he was rummaging the drawers in the bedroom."

"Did you hear a car drive away?"

"No sir, but you see Mike was making such a noise with his barking that I mightn't have heard it."

"And when you got out again through the window all you thought of was running after Mr Casey. In fact you legged it home as hard as you could go."

"Yes sir."

"And when you got home Mr Casey hadn't come in?"

"No sir, but he came in about half an hour later and went straight up to his room. He must have been there last night and seen me, because when he passed me on the stairs this morning he hissed in my ear, 'You young devil! If you don't stop following me about I'll hand you over to the police.'"

"Well, Pat, here are my orders. You're to pretend that you're frightened at what he said and stop following him about, until I give you the word."

"Very good, sir," replied Pat in a dejected tone.

"And now you run away to your dinner and cheer up. I shall have something for you to do in the future." As soon as the door had shut upon the boy Ann looked in.

"Well, what did you make of his story?"

"I believe it. He has been very useful, and he may be even more useful in the future."

"But surely it wasn't Mr Casey that he saw?"

"No, it wasn't. The behaviour of the dog showed that. If you want to know my deductions from his story I will tell you what they are. The man whom he surprised in the bungalow, whoever he was, had come in a car, and when he got out through the window he made straight for that car and lay low in it with his lights switched off until the boy's footsteps died away. Then he drove off."

"And so Casey had nothing to do with it?" said Ann in a flat tone.

"No, except probably as a spectator, for he is still taking a morbid interest in that bungalow."

Chapter Fifteen

DIVISIONAL DETECTIVE INSPECTOR Aitkin had completed his search of the bungalow and was back in his office preparing to go to lunch when his chief came up the stairs two at a time.

"Well, what luck did you have?" he asked.

Aitkin shook his head ruefully. "The only drugs I found in that cursed bungalow consisted of this bottle of aspirin tablets— at least they're labelled aspirin and they look like it. But I did find this." He pushed over to Richardson an antique seal of some red stone set in gold and inscribed with a double E interlaced.

"Where did you find it?"

"It was in this little purse at the back of one of the drawers in which that burglar had been rummaging last night."

"H'm! We'll keep this. It may become important. E was not the dead woman's initial, but I believe you'll find it on one of those bags."

"Yes, on that very expensive bag. This is the one, and the design on the seal is very like that on the bag."

"Label it, and put it in your safe. We may have the luck to come across a letter sealed with it. You've noticed that the little purse is made of the same material as the bag."

"Yes, I see that."

"Did you send in the advertisement inviting owners of the bags to come forward?"

"Yes, but there's scarcely been time yet for any answers. I searched the bungalow for other letters, but without finding any, except a few business ones addressed to Pomeroy. I feel that I've had a blank morning."

"One can never say that in this job of ours. That seal may become a turning point in the case. Now I'll tell you what I've been doing before I go." He described what he had found in the letters. "I'm running up to town now to see those solicitors Jackson and Burke, who have to prove Colter's will."

"You'll find them out at lunch now."

"Yes, but I can play at the same game and catch them when they come back."

When Richardson presented himself at the office of Messrs Jackson and Burke in Southampton Street he was not kept waiting. He was shown into the room of the senior partner, Mr Jackson, who rose to shake hands with him.

"I have been expecting a visit from you, Superintendent, for a day or two."

"I've called about the will of Mr Frederick Colter, who died recently in New Zealand."

Mr Jackson was a man of about sixty—a man who inspired confidence. "As you may know, Mr Colter was a personal friend of mine and his death was a grief to me. He had been exceptionally successful with his sheep run in New Zealand, and he had always kept in touch with me, consulting me about his investments and so forth. He chose to have his will proved in this country and named me as his executor. Steps have already been taken to obtain probate. He had a fairly large sum invested in gilt-edged securities in this country. I suppose that you gentlemen from Scotland Yard know everything, and so it is not necessary for me to tell you the terms of his will."

Richardson smiled. "I came to ask you whether you are satisfied with the proofs of identity brought by Mr Colter's adopted son."

Mr Jackson appeared startled. "Why? Is there any doubt about his identity? He had all his papers in order—the will, his birth certificate, the certificate of death of my old friend Colter, and a personal letter written to me by Colter which was undoubtedly in his handwriting. If there is any reasonable doubt about the authenticity of any of these documents I shall be very glad to produce them for your inspection."

"His niece, Mrs Pomeroy, as you will have seen in the newspapers, was murdered, and I am in charge of the investigation: that is my excuse for taking up your time. One point on which I seek enlightenment is this. Now that Mrs Pomeroy is dead, who becomes her heir?"

"That question is easily answered. We have ascertained that she died intestate, and, therefore, her share will go to her husband for his lifetime. We understand that at the moment he is ill in bed and unable to attend to any business, but that is the position."

"Well, my reason for asking if you are sure of the identity of Edward Maddox is that I have some reason for doubting whether the young man is actually the person he represents himself to be. I have a letter here written by Mr Colter to his niece Stella Pomeroy in which he speaks of the studious tastes of his adopted son."

"Studious?"

"Exactly. I have seen Edward Maddox more than once, and 'studious' is the last word that I should have applied to him. What is your opinion of him?"

"The same as yours. He strikes me as a silly, blustering, ill-mannered young man. I have wondered after every interview with him how my dear old friend Colter could have been attached to him. I think that under the circumstances I should be justified in showing you the documents he produced to me."

He rose and lumbered over to a big safe in the corner of the room and took from it a large official-looking envelope containing papers.

"I suggest that on the face of them these papers are genuine. There can be no question of forgery."

Richardson took each of the papers to the window and held it up to the light. "No, I agree with you, Mr Jackson, there is no sign of any of these having been tampered with. If there is anything wrong with them it is that they are being carried by the wrong man."

"Then you suggest...?"

"I suggest that a cable should be sent to the police in Wellington, or to any responsible correspondent that you may have in Wellington, asking whether Edward Maddox is in charge of Mr Colter's sheep run. We ought to have a reply within a couple of days."

"I forgot another proof of his identity. He came to this office one day with a young man whom he represented as being Mrs Stella Pomeroy's brother."

"I know the man you mean—Arthur Grant, the actor. He was actually her brother."

"Well, Grant professed to have known Maddox in New Zealand, and he vouched for his identity."

"May I ask whether Maddox has been granted any advance upon his expectations as heir to Mr Colter?"

"Yes. He had a great deal to say about the law's delays, and as his certificates of identity seemed unassailable we have been paying him sums of money from week to week. I cannot tell you the exact amount without having the books looked up."

"Well, Maddox is paying Grant's hotel bills and may be providing him with cash besides. He did not strike me as an open-handed young man, and it occurred to me that he feels himself in some way in Grant's power."

"Oh! That's quite a new light. Are you having them watched?"

"I'm having some quiet observation kept upon the three. I ought to mention that there's a third man named Otway with them, and Otway is a person with a police record in New Zealand."

"Indeed. It is, naturally, always the policy of my firm to assist justice. What do you suggest that I should do?"

"I should advise you to go on as you are doing for the next few days. I do not want to have them frightened at this stage of my enquiry. I am expecting to have a report from the man who is keeping them under observation, late this evening, and if there are any new developments I will let you know tomorrow morning. You will be in your office at ten?"

"Yes. Ten always finds me in this chair. Ask for me personally when you ring up."

"And meanwhile you will send the cable?"

"Yes; to my agent in Wellington. You want me simply to ask the question whether Edward Maddox is still in charge of Colter's sheep run."

"Yes, but I should add, 'enquire through police.' That would shorten the delay for the reply by several hours, because there is sure to be a subsidiary police office nearer to the sheep run than Wellington, and the local police would be sure to know. If you have any news before ten o'clock tomorrow morning will you ring me up at New Scotland Yard, Whitehall 121a." The lawyer made a note of the number on his blotting pad.

They parted with expressions of mutual good will. "I hope that my payments to this young man can soon be discontinued," said the lawyer as they shook hands.

Richardson's next visit was to the Public Carriage Office in Scotland Yard. He wanted to see Police Constable Dunstan once more. He had now found that Maddox had a motive for committing the murder. There might have been a will, but was there a way? Evidence must be forthcoming as to what became of those two men when they took a taxi from the docks, and this could be furnished by the young constable, Dunstan. He saw him in the outer office and went to the superintendents' room.

"I want to have a word with one of your young constables, Mr Wilkins," he said to the superintendent of the P.C.O. "May I see him here?"

"Certainly. Do you want to see him alone?"

"Oh no. I only want to put one question to him."

"Take a seat then, and I'll call him in."

The constable greeted Richardson with a smile. "I was just going to ask Mr Wilkins to let me ring you up, sir. We found the taximan, who remembered driving two men from the docks to Snelnar's Restaurant in the Old Kent Road that morning. There they paid him off. We got H. Division to make enquiries at Snelnar's, and they remembered two men who said they came from New Zealand that morning who drove up in a taxi, stopping to breakfast. They were asked whether they had a substantial meal and were told that they had. They did not leave the restaurant until half-past nine."

"Did the people at Snelnar's make any mistake about the day, do you think?"

"No sir. It was the morning when the *Aorangi* berthed at the docks."

"Thank you. I suppose I shall have a report to that effect in writing."

"It will be ready for you this evening, sir." Richardson went to the telephone and called up Milsom once more.

"Hallo! You again—twice in the same day. Things must be humming with you."

"They are. They have come to the point that I must see you late this evening at your flat after you have probed deep into the claim of your young friend to literary tastes."

"You are coming to my flat? But I thought we were to keep ourselves rigidly apart."

"Things have been moving so rapidly that I don't think we need any longer consider the risk of being known to be acquainted. So you can expect me at about ten o'clock."

"You needn't wait until then. I'll get my little one-act play over before dinner, and then you'll come to my flat, where I can give you quite a decent meal. Make it eight o'clock and wait for me if I'm not there."

It was always a great relief to Richardson to find himself alone in the superintendents' room to write his reports, for the business of setting down the facts helped him in forming a comprehensive view of the case as it had progressed so far. The superintendents' room was at this moment a haven of rest, for all his colleagues happened to be out upon enquiries. At this period the reports of C.I.D. officers were written in manuscript and were seldom dictated. The practice was less uneconomical than it sounds, because the reports never left the office and were intended only for the eyes of a superior officer. The result was that the vast accumulation of documents to be found in other public offices was avoided. The disadvantage was that the file belonging to each big case was swollen with half-sheets of foolscap paper—the reports of subordinate officers sent to make subsidiary enquiries. Even in the Criminal Investigation Department there was a rough adherence to the hours of duty in other public departments) in that officers employed in routine duties put on their hats at six o'clock and the stone passages ceased to resound to heavy boots. But since Superintendent Richardson had nothing else to do before a quarter to eight he sat on until the building became as silent as a church; even the telephones were stilled.

At length the hour arrived for him to keep his appointment at Milsom's flat. The ring at the bell produced the host himself, who shook hands with an air of suppressed elation, shut the door carefully behind his guest and pushed up a chair for him.

"I probed that 'studious' brain to the bottom, and I can tell you it took some doing. If I'd been one of those Johnnies who from time to time talk through their hats on the B.B.C. from provincial universities it would have been an easy job, but remember that for me, whose books are 'thrillers' and whose only authors are men and women who aspire to follow in the footsteps of Edgar Wallace, it was necessary to begin with sweating up English literature myself. It was an awful waste of labour, as I found in the first five minutes, because this bloke of ours of 'studious' habits had never even heard of Sir Walter Scott, still less of George Bernard Shaw, and thought that H.G. Wells was the inventor of a cure for the liver."

"How did you introduce the subject?"

"Oh, that wasn't difficult. We ordered the drinks as usual, and then I said to Maddox, 'I suppose you don't get much time for reading over here.' And he said, 'Reading? Do you mean the newspapers? Because I've never read anything else in my life.' At this moment there was an awkward accident: Otway managed to upset Maddox's glass of beer, and when they had mopped it up Grant said, 'I remember when you were a youngster you always had your nose in a book of some kind, generally high-brow stuff.'"

"Then Grant can't be in the swindle—if it is a swindle, as I firmly believe."

"No, I don't believe he is. But Otway was quite equal to the occasion. He said, 'What a memory you have, Ted! It was when you were switched off onto the outdoor work that you had to put aside your reading.' I can tell you, I gave them a doing. I talked of nothing but books until they were thankful to see the back of me. You see I was charged up to the eyes with erudition, and I had to fire it off upon somebody. Now we're not going to have all this work for nothing. When are you going to arrest him for the murder, because I don't want to miss that little entertainment."

"I'm sorry to tell you that, though we are on the track of a swindle, we are no nearer the discovery of the murderer of Mrs Pomeroy than we were a week ago. Every clue seems to melt in our hands when we turn it over. We have got reliable proof that these men were in another part of London altogether at the time of the murder."

"Then all my hard work is thrown away."

"Not at all. It's going to result in the arrest and trial of a couple of swindlers who've come all the way from New Zealand to exploit a fraud. We're only awaiting the reply to a cable which we ought to get tomorrow."

"Well, while I've been overworking my brain here in town what have you been doing down at Ealing?"

"I'll tell you our latest discoveries."

Milsom listened in rapt attention while his friend described the adventure at the bungalow, the discovery of the ladies' handbags and the hopes that he had that these might furnish a fresh clue.

"As is always the case in these complicated enquiries, one spends the first few days in eliminating what appear to be useful clues. This time our efforts have not been wasted, because, while hunting down a murderer, we have come across two swindlers ripe for prosecution."

"Well," said Milsom as his friend rose to go, "I hope you're going to employ me in hunting down the lady who blazons her initials on her vanity bag, always providing that E does not stand for Edith or Emmie, because I have known ladies who answered to both those names and they sent shivers down my spine. I rather fancy myself as a lady-killer."

Chapter Sixteen

HAVING RECEIVED no telephone message from Mr Jackson, the lawyer, by ten o'clock the following morning, Richardson decided to go via Southampton Street on his way down to Ealing. He found the senior partner as good as his word: he was in his chair by that hour.

"You've had no answer yet to your cable, Mr Jackman?"

"No, Mr Richardson, but I'm expecting one any minute. Have you anything to tell me about that young man?"

"The young man of studious habits? Yes, I have. A certain informant who knows him tried last night to interest him in discussing English literature. The young man had never heard of George Bernard Shaw, and he believed H.G. Wells to be an inventor of a cure for the liver. Further, he admitted that he never read anything but newspapers, and his companion upset his glass of beer, which seemed to be a preconcerted signal for covering up lapses on the part of the young man who represents himself as Edward Maddox."

"That certainly suggests that he is an impostor, but we shall know as soon as I receive a reply to my cable."

At that moment a junior clerk entered with a telegram. Mr Jackson, forgetting his usual legal precision of slitting open the envelope and pinning it to the document it contained, tore it open with an impatient finger and read the telegram.

"Listen to this, Mr Richardson. 'Edward Maddox died July thirty-first.' So this young man has been obtaining money from me under false pretences."

"Yes, Mr Jackson, but that may not be the only offence he has committed. He has probably landed in this country under a false name and with false papers. For these offences he could be charged on a summons at once, because I assume that a magistrate might hesitate to grant a warrant, and the offence is not a felony, but a misdemeanour."

"Yes, and the offence of obtaining money from me under false pretences is also a misdemeanour. What do you think our procedure should be? Shall we both apply for summonses and get them heard together?"

"Before applying for the summons I think it would be well if I had an interview with Grant, the elder brother of that murdered woman, who is now living at the expense of the supposed Ted Maddox. He may be able to give me some clue to the real identity of this young impersonator. I can arrange to do this today, and we can apply for the summonses tomorrow morning."

"Certainly. You will require this cablegram as evidence."

"No, Mr Jackson, I shall subpoena one of the cable clerks from the post office to prove the telegram and one of your clerks to prove the receipt. But I'll see Grant first and then communicate with you."

"You don't think Grant will alarm the other two rascals into leaving the country?"

"No, because we shall put their names on the gate."

"You mean...?"

"We shall warn the port officers to stop them and send their passports to Scotland Yard. It may be that he produced his own passport to the port officers. I have knowledge that he was known as Maddox on board the boat coming over. Could he be a relation of the Ted Maddox who died on July thirty-first?"

"That is quite possible. I think that your idea of interviewing Grant is very good, but I assume that you'll be careful to see him apart from the other rascals."

"Yes, I shall send a detective officer from Ealing, who will say that he is required down there to give some information about his dead sister and that he will not be detained for long."

"Then I shall do nothing until I hear from you again." From the office in Southampton Street Richardson drove down to Ealing, where, learning that the detective inspector was busily engaged upstairs, he despatched one of the detective patrols to the Palace Hotel with the message to Grant.

He found cause for regretting that advertisement about ladies' bags. The waiting room downstairs was half filled with impatient ladies. A harassed constable was endeavouring to deal with the applicants in order of arrival, but that did not prevent attempts by the ladies to "jump" their turns. For Inspector Aitkin the task was formidable. He required each applicant to give the colour and the material of her bag and then, if the description corresponded with a bag in his collection, to pick it out from the others. He was not compounded of soft clay, having, as he said, a wife at home, and most of the ladies left the station empty handed. Those who passed his interrogation came away even more indignant than those who had failed, because they valued the contents of their bags as highly as the bags themselves, and the contents were not there.

As Richardson entered the room a pleasant-looking middle-aged woman was being interviewed.

"Well sir," she was saying, "of course it was my own fault. It was in the hat department of Giveen's, and the walls are plastered with notices that you put down your property at your own risk; that the shop is not responsible. But you know how it is in trying on a hat. You must have both your hands free when you go to the glass, so you put down your bag with your hat on top of it and turn to the glass, and when you turn round again your bag's gone. Lord, but there are some dishonest people in the world. But if you gentlemen have been picking up one of these bag thieves it struck me that I ought to come and see whether she had got mine."

She proceeded to give a description of her missing property. Aitkin listened carefully and laid before her one of the bags. She pounced upon it. "Yes sir, that's mine. You see it's the same as the description I gave you, right down to the fastening." She opened it. "Oh, what a shame! The woman who pinched it has taken out everything, and it isn't as if there were valuables, except for the money which I never thought to get back, but you see everything's gone—even the snapshots of my little nieces, which had no value for anybody but me. Well sir, I'm very much obliged to you, I'm sure."

"I'm sorry for the loss of the contents, madam, but you see a thief would naturally destroy any evidence that might bring the theft home to her."

Richardson sat in the background, scrutinizing every claimant as she came in and listening to Aitkin's competent way of handling them. By midday all the bags had been given to their rightful, or pretended, owners, except the costly bag bearing the initial E. No claimant had come forward for that, and none of the claimants were of the class that would carry a bag of that kind.

"I see no claimant has come forward for that expensive bag marked E."

"Not yet, sir, though a description of it was circulated in the list of lost property."

"It is very significant, to my mind, that no one has come forward. There may have been something in it which the owner regarded as compromising. In that case an advertisement will never produce a claimant."

"What do you mean?"

"Well, it might have been drugs, or it might have been a compromising address which the owner would not like the police to have. One can only guess at it, but I can't help feeling that that bag has a strong bearing on our case. Most of the women lost their bags in the same way, by putting them down while they tried on a hat. That was evidently Stella Pomeroy's method of working. Many of the losers said that they made a complaint in the shop at the time. It's possible that the owner of the bag marked E also made a complaint when she first missed it. It will be worth while for you to send round to the big stores, asking whether they have had a complaint in connection with a bag of this description."

"Very good, Superintendent. I will have this done."

"I took the liberty of sending one of your patrols up to the Palace Hotel to bring Grant down to this office to answer one or two questions about his dead sister."

"In connection with the murder, do you mean?"

"No, I want him to give us some information about this man who calls himself Maddox. We don't know at present who he is, because Ted Maddox, who we assumed him to be, died on July thirty-first."

"Then this man's a fraud?"

"To the extent that he poses as Ted Maddox he is, but his name may be Maddox all the same, and I want to question Grant about him. Unfortunately one cannot clear up the murder as easily as that, because we now have evidence that the men who landed from New Zealand on September thirteenth had a perfect alibi for the hour of the murder."

The station sergeant looked in. "The patrol has just arrived with that man Grant, sir. Where will you see him?"

"I'll see him in this room."

"Very good, sir."

While the men were mounting the stairs, Richardson took his seat at the table and assumed a magisterial air.

"Sit down there, Mr Grant. I want to have a heart-to-heart talk with you."

Grant glanced nervously behind him as if looking for support from the patrol who had brought him upstairs, but he found that he was alone with his interrogator, who proceeded: "You know that Mr Colter left half his fortune to your dead sister and that, as she died without making a will, her share will go to her husband for his lifetime."

"Yes, I know, and it's a damned shame. Mr Otway told me that it was the law."

"Oh, is Mr Otway an authority on wills?"

"I don't know that he's exactly an authority, but he's been looking up the law in the case to see whether I couldn't get my whack out of my uncle's estate."

"Your uncle left you nothing? How long is it since you left New Zealand?"

"It must be about fifteen years."

"Was Ted Maddox living with your uncle when you left?"

"Yes, he had just left college."

"He was fond of study, I believe."

"Yes, he was. He brought back a lot of prizes. I know that when my uncle talked to me about him he didn't think that he'd take kindly to farm life."

"After you left New Zealand fifteen years ago, you never saw Ted Maddox again?"

"That's right. I didn't see him again until I met him at the cemetery at my sister's funeral."

"And you found him a good deal changed?"

Richardson was watching him closely and caught the look of awakened caution in his face.

"Everyone changes in fifteen years."

"Tastes and all, do you think?"

"Yes."

"But two years ago Ted Maddox hadn't changed in his tastes. He still loved books."

"How do you know?"

"I know it from letters that your uncle wrote to your sister."

"They say that I ought to have the letters written to my sister."

"Who are they?"

"Why, Ted Maddox and Otway."

"Those letters are the legal property of your sister's husband, her next of kin. You will have to apply to him."

"What I don't understand is why you've had me brought down here to be questioned like this. Have you got anything against me, because if you have you had better tell me so outright."

"I've nothing against you. All I want from you is that you should help the cause of justice by answering one question quite truthfully. Are you satisfied in your own mind that Maddox is actually the Ted Maddox whom you knew at your uncle's sheep run in New Zealand?"

"Well, I couldn't swear that he isn't."

"But on the other hand you couldn't swear that he is. Is that it?"

"Yes, if you put it that way, I suppose it is."

"Have you ever mentioned your doubts to him?"

"Not in so many words, because Otway is always there, and whenever I seem to be getting near the point he cuts in and talks about Ted's loss of memory and then he shoves ten pounds into my hand and says, 'You forget about his loss of memory.' And mind you, I can't be sure, because a boy of sixteen does change by the time he's thirty-one."

"Do you know why your uncle adopted Ted Maddox?"

"Well, he was the son of an old friend, John Maddox, who hadn't been so successful as my uncle, and he was one of a large family, while my uncle had no son. Have you any reason for doubting that he is Ted Maddox?"

This was a difficult question for Richardson to answer, for if he replied in the affirmative what he said would almost certainly be passed on to the two rascals staying at the Palace Hotel. He replied by asking another question.

"Your sister did not leave New Zealand at the same time that you did?"

"No, not until five years later. You see your suspicion must be wrong, because the first thing that Ted Maddox did was to go down to Ealing with his adopted father's will to show it to my sister, and he must have known that she would recognize him at once."

The obvious answer would have been to say that the object in visiting the heiress was to persuade her to become an accomplice in the deception, but Richardson did not suggest this to his visitor.

"I don't know that I need detain you any longer, Mr Grant," he said, half rising from his seat. "But I'd like you to keep this conversation that we've had confidential. You can say that I'd sent for you to ask whether your sister had a hasty temper and other questions of that sort."

"Well, as we're talking quite confidentially, I think I ought to tell you that neither Maddox nor Otway intends to go back to New Zealand. All they're waiting for is to get the money from those solicitors and then slip off with it to South America."

By this time Richardson felt that there was little more to be learned about the character of the man before him. He was no criminal in intent, but he was a poor, weak-willed creature who would always take the line of least resistance. He decided that the moment had come for telling him the truth, but in such a way that even if he divulged it to the two men at the hotel there would be no danger of their escaping justice.

"Now, Mr Grant, you've been so frank with me that I feel that I ought to tell you the truth. Ted Maddox died on the thirty-first of July last, and this Maddox is probably his brother."

The look of astonishment on Grant's face was an assurance that this was news to him and that he was in no way implicated in the imposture.

"Ted Maddox dead! That explains a lot that I couldn't understand, but it's Otway who's got the brains: Maddox does nothing without consulting him first. And all this money they've been getting from the lawyers...what's going to happen about that?"

"That's easy to answer. The lawyers are going to proceed against Maddox for obtaining money under false pretences."

"If they got to know that they'd be off to South America by the next boat."

"No they wouldn't. The police at every port of embarkation are on the lookout for them. They'll have to stay here to answer the charge which is being made against them, or at any rate one of them, by the solicitor. All you have to do, Mr Grant, is to keep your mouth shut and carry on for a day or so as usual."

Chapter Seventeen

It was obvious that the next step to be taken was to see Mr Jackson, the solicitor, again and tell him that as it appeared probable that Maddox had landed with a legal passport of his own, the police had no ground for taking out a summons against him, whereas in respect of obtaining money under false pretences, the solicitors had a clear right of action. Richardson decided to give Mr Jackson time to return from luncheon before calling. When he saw him early in the afternoon it was decided between them that Mr Jackson should obtain a summons immediately. Then arose the question whether the information should include Otway as aiding and abetting the fraud.

"The difficulty in Otway's case," suggested Richardson, "is that he may plead that he too was a victim of the fraud; that he had simply accepted the story of a fellow traveller and had had no means of checking it. Personally I believe that Otway was at the bottom of the fraud. He knew that if Maddox had presented himself as the elder of the surviving brothers of Ted Maddox he would have received only one seventh of his brother's fortune as his share, but by passing himself off as that dead brother he would get the lot. In looking up my reports I see that the purser of the Aorangi described how Maddox behaved on the voyage. At the beginning he had come into a modest fortune, but the fortune grew until when they were nearing England he had become something approaching a millionaire. At the time I thought that this was merely due to his bombastic character, but now I have come round to the belief that it was owing to suggestions made by Otway. I presume that the late Mr Colter's personal property in England amounts to a considerable sum, because I learn from Grant that their intention is to go to South America and not to return to New Zealand."

"Mr Colter had investments in gilt-edged securities amounting to at least two hundred thousand pounds. After what you have just told me, Mr Richardson, I shall issue a summons for both the men."

As he left the office Richardson had to remind himself that in tracking down these minor rascals he was not getting on with his real preoccupation—the discovery of the murderer. These two could now be left to the mercies of Mr Jackson, but he reflected ruefully that they were going to be no help to him.

In view of certain passages in Casey's letters there were questions to ask him, but a newspaper office was certainly not the place for an interview of that description. He would have to wait and send for him as he did before. This time, in view of the references to the "dangerous game" he was playing with the dead woman, there was fresh material for inviting him to a second interview and the invitation need not be too politely worded. Then from Casey his thoughts wandered to Ann Pomeroy, who had always suspected the Irishman. Was it woman's intuition, or some gift that had been denied to him? He himself did not believe that Casey was the actual murderer, but it was clear from the correspondence that he had been engaged in some illicit business with the dead woman. Ann Pomeroy had been right in suspecting from the very beginning that Casey was at the bottom of the mystery, and then the memory of those clear grey eyes set his thoughts wandering, and he brought himself up with a start on discovering that he, a staid detective officer, had allowed his feet to carry him two whole streets out of his way while his thoughts were filled with Ann Pomeroy.

It is not often that a superintendent has time to kill during an afternoon, but on this day Richardson found himself free for the afternoon to write his report at the Central Office and clear up a number of small points that had arisen during his investigation. He was at his writing table when Mr Beckett, the Chief Constable, looked in.

"Oh! It's not often that one finds you at your table in these days, and it's not very often that one has the opportunity of reading your handwriting. How are you getting on with that Ealing murder case?"

"Not very fast, Mr Beckett, I'm sorry to say. It's a complicated kind of case, and one after another the persons suspected have succeeded in producing alibis. It's entailing a lot of work, but it's not been altogether wasted. Two of the suspects are being prosecuted on a charge of fraud."

"Do you want help? I fancy you're not finding D.D. Inspector Aitkin much good to you."

"Oh, he's all right, sir. He's doing a lot of patient investigation, but I confess that it's an extraordinarily difficult case. There is documentary evidence that the dead woman was engaged in some unlawful business, and I hope that by this evening I shall know what it was. It may turn out to be important in giving us a clue towards finding out who was the murderer."

"Well, there's one thing to guard against. We can't afford to make another arrest and then have to let the man go."

"No sir. We must avoid that at all costs."

The time passes quickly when reports have to be written. Richardson realized with a start that if he was to make an appointment with Casey he must either try to lure him to New Scotland Yard or to the police station at Ealing. He decided on the latter course and resolved to despatch a patrol to head him off from his lodgings when he returned from town. For this purpose he selected Sergeant Hammett as being the most likely man to use the fist in the velvet glove successfully.

He found himself comfortably seated in the divisional detective inspector's office about the time when Casey was likely to arrive. He must have returned by an earlier train than usual that evening, for Richardson's quick ear soon caught the sound of an Irish accent on the stairs. As far as he could judge the Irishman was still undeflated in his tone. Bluff was again to be his armour against inconvenient questions.

"Sit down, Mr Casey."

"If it's all the same to you. I'd rather stand."

"That is just as you please. Since I saw you last I have been reading pertain correspondence that passed between you and the late Mrs Pomeroy."

"You police seem to spend your time in reading other people's correspondence. Don't you find it a dirty business?"

"In your case I confess that I did, but unhappily we are condemned to do that, though in many cases the correspondence produces a feeling of nausea. I speak in a general way; I do not specify the correspondence I am thinking of. Let us turn to your own letters written to the late Mrs Pomeroy."

"Why, you'd read those letters before I saw you last."

"I hadn't studied them. At that time I thought that the words 'dangerous game we are playing' might refer only to Mrs Pomeroy's infidelities under the nose of her husband; now, in the light of what I have since heard, they seem to take on a different significance, and I want you to throw light on the phrase 'dangerous game.'"

"You put a name to it just now. Marital infidelities, or words to that effect."

"I suggest to you that the words meant more than that—that you were associated with this woman in some enterprise that would have cost you both dear if it had become known. I want you, if you can, to explain those words away."

"In other words you want me to do your work for you. I've nothing to conceal. Supposing that I get a written guarantee of immunity from you, or a verbal assurance in the presence of a witness of my own that nothing I say will be used against me? You can take it or leave it."

"You admit, then, that you have been engaged in some unlawful enterprise?"

"I admit nothing, but I daresay that under the conditions I have specified I might admit quite a lot that the police have been too stupid to find out for themselves. The interesting thing to me is that I've always understood that you British police prided yourselves on not using the third degree to extort confessions. In fact, that the practice was strictly forbidden."

Richardson laughed at his effrontery. "I invited you here to explain a phrase used by you in a letter. You are a perfectly free agent; you can leave this room and walk out into the street whenever you like."

"Thank you. I will." And the young man clattered down the stairs. Richardson was on the point of signalling to the station sergeant to stop him when the footsteps on the stairs hesitated, turned and began to ascend again. The sleek head was thrust in at the door.

"You won't forget what I told you—that the 'dangerous game' meant marital infidelity?"

"No, Mr Casey, I won't forget that you said so. By the way, have you lost an Irish shilling?"

This unexpected question did throw the young man off his balance for a moment.

"I may have. Why do you ask?"

"Because one of your Irish shillings has been picked up in a most unexpected place." He could not avoid marking the look of suspicion and alarm on his visitor's face. "Now here's a bargain, Mr Casey. You tell me the real meaning of those words, 'dangerous game,' and I'll tell you where that Irish shilling was found."

The hasty temper of the Irishman blazed up. "You're trying to blackmail me into making a confession."

"Blackmail is an ugly word, Mr Casey. I'm trying to get the truth out of you by perfectly legitimate questions." But even as he was speaking the truth flashed across Richardson's mind. Unconsciously Casey had supplied the explanation: the dangerous game the two had been playing was blackmail. For the moment he felt that he could afford to let the man go while he thought over the evidence in the most difficult of all crimes that confront detective officers.

"Well, good night, Mr Casey. I don't feel that our interview has been entirely wasted. When you do feel inclined to enlighten me further, I shall be very glad to see you."

Inspector Aitkin was at that moment in the sergeant's room discussing what was to be done about a complaint of shoplifting. He looked up as Richardson entered and obeyed a signal to follow him into his own room.

"We've got one step further, I think, Mr Aitkin. The 'dangerous game' referred to in that letter I told you about was blackmail."

"Good heavens! As if we hadn't got enough on our hands without blackmail. I remember being told in the detective class that it was the most difficult of all crimes to bring home, because the victim would do anything rather than come forward."

"You're quite right. It is the most difficult of all crimes, because almost invariably there is a modicum of truth in the threatened exposure, and the victim thinks that people will always believe the worst of him. The blackmail has to go very far before the worm turns, and when he does turn he is in a worse position than ever: his friends say that there must have been something in it if he paid hush money, and those who refuse to believe it regard him as a coward."

"But hasn't there been a lull in blackmailing since the lord chief justice dealt with that gang of Taylor and those other rascals?"

"Yes, a life sentence and so on down the scale does make criminals think twice before they engage in the game. There has been a lull in prosecutions, no doubt, but how many of the little tin gods in provincial towns submit to blackmail of a minor kind rather than have their names dragged in the mud when they are aspiring to municipal honours or are preachers in nonconformist chapels and the like? In those little communities the blackmailer finds his victims. He does not seek a private interview and demand hush money: he comes forward as an indignant supporter who will expend his last shilling in defending the honour of the victim."

"But how is this new discovery going to help us in the question of the murder, Mr Richardson?"

"That we cannot guess as yet, only we must bear in mind that when people feel the pinch of the blackmailer their instinct is to silence him, and there is always one alternative to buying him off. In thinking over the practices of that dead woman I cannot forget that expensive-looking bag that you found bearing the initial E, together with that burglary which was discovered by the Coxon boy. Let us put two and two together in the form of conjecture. Stella Pomeroy stole that bag, and in the bag she found something so compromising that she and Casey used it as material for blackmail. The victim of the blackmail, or someone acting for her, came down the other evening and tried to find that bag with its contents. Now, is it possible that they had already tried—on the morning of the murder?"

"Well, I've got every man I can spare going round the big stores to discover who was the owner of that bag."

"And I shall just have time to run up to the Pomeroys' house to ask Mr Pomeroy whether his wife had received any money from unexplained sources."

It might have been considered strange that when he rang the bell at the house of Pomeroy senior he should have asked the little maid not for Mr Miles Pomeroy, but for Miss Ann. He was shown immediately into the little den off the front hall which he was coming to know so well. Ann rose from her desk.

"Have you brought any fresh news?"

"No, but I've called to ask Mr Pomeroy a question. Is he well enough to see me?"

"I think so. Is it a question that will worry him much?"

"Well, it's a question that doesn't reflect credit on his dead wife. I remember when we first met that you believed Casey to be the guilty person. Your woman's intuition was right up to a point. He was guilty, not of the murder, but of another crime in which he was associated with the dead woman. I know that I can trust you." He explained briefly his new suspicions of what Casey had described as a "dangerous game."

"Thank you for trusting me," said Ann. There was a new air of friendly confidence in her tone. "I don't think that you need have any fear of asking Miles questions. You see, for months past he was thinking of leaving her: there was no sentiment left between them. How could there be? I'll go and fetch him."

Miles Pomeroy was looking far better in health than Richardson had seen him up to the present.

"I'm sorry to keep bothering you, Mr Pomeroy, but there are one or two questions that I must ask you. Had your wife a separate banking account?"

"Yes, I believe she opened one quite recently, but I've made no enquiries from the manager as to what her credit amounted to."

"Do you know where she kept her chequebook and passbook; we have found no trace of them in the bungalow."

"I haven't the slightest idea. I should have thought that you would find them in her writing desk."

"No. We have looked through the drawers very carefully. Will you give me the name of the bank?"

"It was the Ealing branch of the National Deposit."

"Thank you very much, Mr Pomeroy. I can ascertain her balance from the bank manager."

He rose to go, but at that moment the door was pushed open and Ann appeared with a tray.

"You are not going without some of my coffee, Mr Richardson. Remember, you told me that it was the best coffee you had tasted since you were in France."

And Richardson the detective became Richardson the mere man once more.

Chapter Eighteen

RICHARDSON's first visit next morning was to the manager of the local branch of the National Deposit Bank. When he was alone with that functionary he explained that he had called for information about the account of the late Mrs Stella Pomeroy. The manager at once became alert.

"I was wondering how soon one of you gentlemen would be calling upon me about that account. It was opened under rather peculiar circumstances only about a month ago. The lady insisted on having a private interview with me, and was particular in asking whether her account and the amount of her balance would be kept in strict confidence and not divulged to any person who might ask about it. She then put down on this table three bundles of treasury notes, which were counted and found to be bundles of fifty. I knew, of course, that her husband was employed by a London bank, and I thought it a little odd that she should have a separate account with us, but she explained that she was working —she did not say at what—and wished to keep what she earned separate. A day or two before her death she came in and again asked to see me. It was only to add another fifty pounds to her balance."

"Was this last payment also made in one-pound treasury notes?"

"Yes. It was the air of mystery about her visits that made me take a special interest in the case. I remember wondering what sort of work she was doing that brought in money like this, and why it was not paid by cheque. However, there it is, and we hold it at the disposal of her heir-at-law."

"That will be her husband. Did she deposit any papers with you?"

"Nothing but the money that I have told you of."

"Thank you very much for the information."

At the police station Richardson found Inspector Aitkin going over the reports of the officers whom he had sent round the big stores to trace the bag.

"I've just come from the local bank, Mr. Aitkin. The manager gave me very significant information about the dead woman's account. It was opened only about a month ago, and altogether two hundred pounds had been paid in—all in one-pound treasury notes. It is, as you know, the practice of blackmailers to demand payment in this form and not in Bank of England notes, because these can be traced, whereas there is no means of tracing treasury notes."

"She was a cunning woman, Mr Richardson."

"Or rather she had a cunning man behind her."

"I've been going through the reports of the men I sent round the big stores to trace the loss of that bag. I told them to ask if the loss of such a bag had been reported. I thought that that was an easier way to begin with than trying to trace where it was bought. But so far I've come across nothing useful."

"While you're looking through those papers I should like to use your telephone."

"Certainly, sir."

Richardson rang up Mr Jackson in Southampton Street.

"Good morning, Mr Jackson. This is Superintendent Richardson speaking. Have you taken any steps regarding those men we were talking about yesterday?...Oh, then the summonses will be served on them this morning...I wonder whether they will try to do a bolt. I think that it might be well for one of my people to keep an eye upon them...I'll put that in train at once."

He turned to Aitkin and explained to him what had happened. "Is Sergeant Hammett at liberty just now?"

"Well, we've got our hands pretty full, sir."

"But this wouldn't take him long. It is only to see whether those two men, Maddox and Otway, leave the Palace Hotel this afternoon, follow them to the railway station and note where they book to. A summons is to be served on them this morning, and it's possible that they may try to do a bunk. Their names have been sent to the port officers, but one never knows whether a man might not slip through."

"Oh, we can spare Hammett for that. He's in the sergeant's room now, if you care to give him the order." When Richardson returned from the sergeant's room Aitkin said, "Here is something that started with promise but ended in nothing. At Carter's Stores a lady complained that her bag had been stolen, and her description of it would tally with the bag we have in that cupboard. The officer went to the house, but the lady thanked him and said that she had recovered her bag. She did not say how."

"Who was the officer?"

"Sergeant Wilbraham, sir."

"Let me have a look at his report."

"I have it here, sir."

Richardson read it aloud:

"In accordance with my instructions I called at Carter's Stores with a description of one of the bags shown to me in this office and was conducted to the basement, where the complaint office is situated. I described the bag; the books were searched, and l was shown an entry containing a close description of the bag marked E. I was allowed to take the name and address of complainant, Mrs Esther, 9 Parkside Mansions. I called on this lady, but she informed me that her bag had been recovered.

"E. WILBRAHIM

"Sergeant"

"I don't feel quite satisfied about this lady," said Richardson, "and yet I don't see that Sergeant Wilbraham could have pressed his question any farther. Is he within call?"

"I think so, sir. I'll look into the sergeant's room."

Aitkin returned a moment later, bringing Sergeant Wilbraham with him.

"I've just been reading your report about your visit to that Mrs Esther," said Richardson. "What was the demeanour of the lady when you told her that we had recovered her bag?"

"She seemed startled, sir, and very uncomfortable."

"And she said in so many words that she had recovered her bag. You hadn't given her a description of it?"

"Oh no, sir. I was going to leave it to her to give the description."

"What sort of lady was she?"

"I understand from enquiries I have made that her husband is a member of the stock exchange and very well-to-do."

"Did she strike you as the sort of person who might be carrying on a flirtation behind her husband's back?"

Sergeant Wilbraham weighed the suggestion. "Yes sir. She was a flashy kind of lady, all made up with red polished fingernails, the sort that would go out into society and play cards and go to dances."

"Do you think she was straightforward in her answers?"

"No sir, I can't say that. She was very anxious to get rid of me."

Richardson decided that this was clearly a case where it might be useful to have a personal interview with the lady. He himself believed that she was the owner of that bag, and he wished to know her reason for not wishing to reclaim her property. He had time before lunch to go and visit Parkside Mansions.

He was admitted without delay to the presence of a rather good-looking young woman. She adopted at first an attitude of annoyance.

"You are the second police officer who has called to see me about some bag you have found. What is all the fuss about?"

Richardson assumed his suavest manner. "It's quite simple, madam. The bag has come into our possession, and, believing it to be yours, we want to restore it to its rightful owner."

"But I have already told one of your men that it wasn't mine. There must be hundreds of such bags. I must really ask you to put a stop to this annoyance."

Richardson was quick to notice that beneath this attitude of haughty annoyance there was fear. His manner became more suave than ever.

"You mustn't blame us for being overzealous in the interests of the people we are bound to protect. All we want is to see that lost property is restored to its rightful owners."

"I quite see that." She became more at her case, thinking that she had successfully bluffed him. Her tone was now amiable. "Well, all I can do is to thank you for calling; but you do understand, don't you, that that bag doesn't belong to me? Why, my bag had ivory mountings, not gold, and, as I told you, I've recovered it."

She had overacted her part. Richardson knew already that Sergeant Wilbraham had never described to her the bag for which he was seeking the owner. For the moment he decided to let her think that her bluff had succeeded. He took his leave amiably and made for the car park just beyond the Serpentine Bridge.

On the way down to Ealing his thoughts were busy. He was satisfied in his own mind that the little Jewess had been lying to him. The bag was hers, and it had contained something compromising which might or might not bear indirectly upon the murder of Stella Pomeroy. It was useless to conjecture what it might have been, but what did appear certain to him was that she had been paying blackmail to Stella Pomeroy and her confederate and was very anxious to deny her ownership of the bag.

When he related to Aitkin how he had fared with the lady at Parkside Mansions the comment of his colleague was characteristic.

"Women are the very devil when they start these games, and when a woman once starts lying she'll deceive the Recording Angel himself."

"Well, we must find out more about her. The question is, who is the best man to employ?"

"Hammett would be the man, but he's up in town now, watching those fellows in the Palace Hotel. If you want him for Parkside Mansions I'll have to release him from the job he's employed on down here."

"I wish you would. I want your best man for this particular enquiry."

"Very well, sir. He's sure to telephone at one o'clock to say how things are going, and I'll recall him. I've another man who can do the job at the Palace Hotel."

"It's nearly one now; I'll wait until you get your call."

The telephone bell rang. "Talk of the devil," said Aitkin, taking up the receiver, but it was a woman's voice that spoke.

"Is that Mr Richardson?"

"No, miss, but he is here." He handed the receiver to his superintendent.

"Who's speaking?"

"Ann Pomeroy. I'm sorry to worry you at such an hour, but I must see you. Could you come down here, or shall I come up?"

"I have the car with me: it will be simpler and quicker if I come down to you."

He turned to Aitkin. "Miss Pomeroy has something fresh to tell me. You had better go to lunch as soon as you've heard from Hammett, and I'll be back here in time to give Hammett his new instructions."

"Very good, sir." Aitkin refrained from suggesting that his chief might have listened to Miss Pomeroy's news over the telephone.

Ann must have been on the lookout for the car: the door opened as it drew up.

"Oh, I'm so glad you've come," said the girl. "I've had a visit from Mr Grant this morning. Come into my den, and I'll tell you about it. He came to ask if he could be allowed to visit the bungalow to take some little object away as a memento of his dead sister. At first I felt no suspicion: he struck me as a sentimental sort of person who might have this desire; but his manner was so nervous that I became convinced that he was simply acting as a mouthpiece for others. I didn't refuse him; I told him that I had the key and that I would come down with him. Evidently this was not what he wanted. He had planned to get admitted to the house alone, but he couldn't well refuse my offer to go with him, and we went down together. The actor in him came out—the third-class actor who always tends to overact his part. He produced what appeared to be real tears when he found himself in the house. He tried every artifice to gain admission to the bedroom by himself, but I stuck to him like a leech under the pretence of making helpful suggestions."

"Such as...?"

"'Well, he faltered out that he would like something that she had used every day. I suggested something off the writing desk—her fountain pen. But that didn't seem to meet the case, and in the end he came out with his real desire, which was to have her handbag. There I was on strong ground, knowing that they were all in your possession. I assented cheerfully and said, 'Let's look for one.' When the search proved useless he contented himself with taking her fountain pen. He apologized for the trouble he had given me and left. But the fact that he wanted a handbag seemed to me a thing that you ought to know as soon as possible.'"

"It thickens the plot. He must have been sent by Otway or Maddox, and now I know that they are in it I feel more hopeful, because steps have already been taken to deal with those two gentlemen."

Ann's eyes were gleaming. "I shall have to make a confession to you, Mr Richardson. This case is fast becoming an obsession with me. I find that I'm neglecting a lot of my household duties and my writing for the magazines, but I'm getting some real material for my fiction."

Richardson laughed. "I've been thinking for some days that this case ought to appear in the official records as Miss Ann Pomeroy's case. At any rate you've earned the right to be told how it progresses, and I shall keep you informed. But now I mustn't keep you any longer from your lunch."

Instead of returning to the business part of Ealing for his own lunch, Richardson went back to the police station to see whether there had been any message from Hammett. He found a note which Aitkin had given to the station sergeant telling him that Sergeant Wilbraham had set out to relieve Hammett, who might be expected to arrive at any moment. He decided to postpone his own lunch until Hammett did arrive. He had not long to wait. A few minutes later he heard the sergeant's step upon the stairs.

"I understand, sir, from Sergeant Wilbraham that you want to see me."

"I do. Did you hand over your observation to Sergeant Wilbraham?"

"Yes sir; all is in order. The two men are still in the hotel and hadn't given notice at the desk that they were leaving when Sergeant Wilbraham took over from me. I introduced him to the hotel porter, who can be trusted thoroughly. If they should give up their rooms he will follow them to the station, note where they book their tickets to and phone down to us. This would give ample time for a description of the men to be telephoned to the port officials."

"I've got a rather delicate enquiry for you. I want you to find out all you can about a Mrs Esther of 9 Parkside Mansions. I have reason for believing that she was the owner of that ornamental bag found in the bungalow where the murder was committed, and that she is now being blackmailed about something that was found in her bag. Consequently, like all victims of blackmail, she won't take us into her confidence. She is thoroughly frightened, and it will be extremely difficult to get any information direct from her. You'll have to be especially discreet, because she's already had two police visits about that bag—the last one from me—and naturally she is now very suspicious of the police."

"I quite understand, sir, but I think I know how I can tackle the job."

"I think that you were the officer who was with D. D. Inspector Aitkin when that bungalow murder was discovered."

"Yes sir, I was."

"Well, you will be interested to know that this enquiry you are undertaking is indirectly connected with that murder."

Chapter Nineteen

AT TWO FORTY-FIVE Wilbraham, who was drinking a modest coffee in the hotel lounge, received a wordless signal from the hall porter indicating that his two charges were on the move. He strolled into the entrance hall, where he had a view of the two men paying their bill at the desk. The porter with their modest luggage emerged from the luggage room. Wilbraham timed his movements to arrive on the pavement at the very moment when the two came out and gave the taximan the direction of Euston Station. Having in his pocket the hours of departure of every train from the London termini, he found that by taking a tube train to Euston he would arrive before them. There was, of course, the risk that they might give their taxi a change of address en route, but that had to be faced. He was in the booking office at Euston in ample time to see the passengers departing for the North and among them the two men whom he had been watching. Quite naturally he fell in behind them in the queue at the ticket office and heard them book to Liverpool. He had now to decide what to do. They were under summons to appear at Bow Street on the following morning. Clearly they were going to try to put themselves out of the jurisdiction of the court, but he had no legal power to control their movements before the court sat. If he did so they might plead that they were going to Liverpool only for the night and intended to return in time for the court sittings. He looked at the clock; there was still twelve minutes, time enough to telephone to Ealing for instructions. Fortunately he was put into direct communication with Superintendent Richardson, whose answer came clearly.

"Even though we may feel sure that these men will attempt to escape out of the jurisdiction of the court it would be safer not to detain them. I shall ask the Liverpool police to keep them under observation and detain them if they attempt to embark on an ocean-going liner."

"Thank you, sir. Then there's nothing more for me to do here?"

"No, you can return to duty here."

Calling up the operator, Richardson asked for the phone number of the Liverpool police and gave the names and descriptions of the two fugitives.

"These men will arrive from Euston at six fifty-five. Both are under summons to appear at Bow Street on a misdemeanour charge, and probably they have gone to Liverpool with the intention of escaping out of the jurisdiction. It is very desirable that the attention of the port officer should be called to them."

"Right, sir. That shall be done."

"I should like to hear the result, if you will phone a message to Superintendent Richardson at the Yard. As far as is known they have not yet booked their passage."

"Very good, sir." The superintendent knew the efficiency of the Liverpool force, whose members combined stature and bulk with brain.

A bulky, typed letter had been put into his hands when he entered the office, and he had not yet had time to open it. He glanced at the signature and saw that it was from Jim Milsom, who, as he felt on his conscience, had been rather neglected of late. It was, as he saw, a very creditable travesty of an official police report beginning, "Acting on instructions, I picked up Smith and Robinson and followed them," and so on. With it was a covering letter.

DEAR SUPERINTENDENT:

As you have seen fit to ignore my existence for nearly forty-eight hours I send you the enclosed report of my movements.

It was true. Poor Jim Milsom had been ignored, but ten minutes ago Richardson had been on the point of ringing him up to ask him to refresh his memory about the stranger whom he had seen in the gambling room signalling to Otway. Perhaps he would find what he wanted in this report. Although written in his friend's usual jocular style, it gave a graphic account of what had happened in the gambling room. He described how the man, who looked like one who had passed through a public school and knew how to comport himself in such circles, had first engaged Otway's attention; the flash of recognition that had passed between the two; and the subtle movement by which Otway had indicated Maddox for the stranger's attention.

For some time Richardson pondered over the report and arrived at last at a decision. He wrote a note to Jim Milsom telling him that he would call for him at his flat at nine-thirty on the following morning. He would have liked to get the business done that same afternoon, but he had to wait for the message from the Liverpool police. He felt that the jigsaw puzzle was beginning to take its proper shape, though there were still a good many pieces missing. It was as well to have all the pieces under his fingers before he made his final moves. He rang up the Palace Hotel to ask whether a gentleman named Grant was still staying at the hotel. On learning that he was, he asked that he might be brought to the phone to speak to a Mr Richardson. There was some delay, and when at last he heard Grant's voice it was charged with some emotion, probably fear.

"I wanted to speak to Mr. Maddox, but they tell me he has left the hotel."

"Yes, but only for a day or two; he and his friend were called up to Liverpool, but they'll soon be back. They wouldn't hear of my leaving the hotel. They told me to reply to all the calls that might come for them and tell enquirers that they would be back in a day or two."

"They left no address?"

"No, none. They said that if the business was very pressing I was to see to it."

"Perhaps you can give me the answer to the question I was going to ask them. Is the bag that they sent you to get for them a black bag with gold mountings and the initial E?"

"Yes," and then, having been taken off his guard, he resumed in an agitated voice, "Oh no. They didn't want any bag at all. It was I who wanted it."

"Well, if you know anyone who wants a bag like that just send him to me."

There was no answer. Apparently Grant must have dropped the receiver in fear that he might commit himself again.

Richardson continued writing his report until the telephone bell rang. It was a message from Liverpool which had been switched over by the operators in New Scotland Yard to Ealing.

"This is a message from the chief constable, Liverpool, to Superintendent Richardson."

"Richardson speaking."

"The two men, the subjects of your telephone message, were followed to the office of the steamship company running to South America. They booked first-class passages to Buenos Aires. The port officers have been warned to prevent them from leaving. The boat sails tomorrow; they have taken rooms at the Mariposa Hotel for the night."

"Thank you," said Richardson. "As they are summoned to appear at Bow Street at eleven o'clock to-morrow morning, they can be arrested and sent down to London at that hour on a charge of failing to obey the summons."

There was still one thing to wait for—the report of Sergeant Hammett, who had been making enquiries at the flat in Parkside Mansions. He might not have discovered very much in one afternoon, but he was worth waiting for. He was the type of officer who would always have something interesting to report at the end of his day's work. Fortunately Richardson had not long to wait. He heard Hammett's step upon the stairs and headed him off at the door of Inspector Aitkin's room.

"Come in here, Sergeant, and tell me what luck you've had."

"Not very much, sir, so far. It appears that Mrs Esther's husband, a member of the stock exchange, is very generous to her in the matter of expensive presents, but that he keeps her rather short of money for a lady in her position. She has become a confirmed bridge player, and all goes well when she is winning; but when bad luck sets in she is hard put to it to pay her losses. Her maid, with whom I was successful in getting on confidential terms, told me that she was beside herself some weeks ago at some heavy debts she had incurred at a bridge club where they play for very high stakes, but she contrived in some way to pay them."

"Did you find out the name of the bridge club?"

"Yes sir—the Worthing, in Curzon Street—but she doesn't go there now. Her husband found it out and stopped her, and from what the maid told me it was time he did. It had become a passion. I haven't yet broached the subject of her handbag, because I want to be a little more certain about the character of the maid before I do."

"Quite right. It's no good hurrying things. You can carry on again tomorrow, because the D.D. Inspector has assigned that case of yours in Ealing to another officer."

When Richardson arrived at his friend Milsom's flat at nine o'clock next morning he found him fully dressed and snatching a hasty breakfast.

"There are limits to the cause of justice, my friend. Here am I dragged out of bed before my last dream was finished; forced into my tub half an hour before my usual time; left no interval for soaking in warm water according to the doctor's orders, and forced to stuff myself with sausage before my appetite has recovered from the shock. What in heaven's name is it all about?"

"I want you to come with me to New Scotland Yard. I have my car waiting down below."

"What am I to do when I get there?"

"I'll tell you while you are putting on your coat. There's a room upstairs where the photographs of criminals can be examined. It is called the crime index room. All the criminals who practise one particular method of crime are filed together in big albums."

"What fun!"

"Do you mean for the criminal or for the searcher?"

"Not, I imagine, for the criminal. But which of my numerous criminal friends do you want me to recognize?"

"Well, you remember that night when Otway and his pal Maddox took you to a gambling hell near Piccadilly Circus?"

"Shall I ever forget it? Bah! The concentrated villainy of Central Europe and the Balkans was overpowering."

"Do you think you would be good at recognizing particular men from their photographs?"

"Try me."

"Well, I'm going to try you. The man I want you to pick out is the man whom you saw signalling to Otway and to whom Otway pointed out Maddox."

"Oh, I'd know that blighter anywhere from his photograph. He had sahib written all over him, but he looked a dissipated bloke as far as features were concerned."

"Very good. Then that's the man I want you to look for."

"Righto! Lead me to your portrait gallery."

They sped down Whitehall and went up to the second floor in the lift. Richardson led the way to what was called, for want of a better name, the crime index room. Here Milsom was introduced to an enthusiast, Sergeant Thoms, whose ingenuity had really founded the system that had been already in embryo, but was now extended. It was based upon the fact that criminals tend always to commit their crimes in the same way, because when a method has been successful they lack the imagination to break out in a new line. And so the various methods—smash-and-grab raids, cat burglary, confidence tricks, larceny by trick, and all the minor varieties of modern crime—are filed in separate pigeonholes, each having a page or two in a gigantic photograph album.

"Here is a case for you, Sergeant Thoms. We are looking for a broken-down gentleman who picks up a precarious living by blackmail."

The sergeant's face lighted up. He looked like a terrier at the word "rats."

"Yes sir, we've quite a fine collection of blackmailers, though I says it as shouldn't."

He brought down a bundle of sheets kept flat between boards tightly strapped together. There must have been more than two hundred of them.

"I suppose you can't give me approximately the date of his conviction, sir?" asked the sergeant.

"The trouble is that I don't know whether he has ever been convicted."

The sergeant's face fell. He looked as deflated as a terrier who finds that the rat is merely a clockwork toy.

"I suggest," said Richardson, "that you show this gentleman photographs not only of blackmailers but of frequenters of gambling dens."

"Right, sir," said Sergeant Thoms, bending under the weight of a vast album carrying sixty-four photographs to the page. This he laid out on the table and turned over the pages until he came to page sixty-eight—blackmailers. "The trouble is, sir, that only perhaps one in fifty of the men who practise blackmail get caught. People are so shy about coming forward to prosecute."

"In case the peccadilloes of their youth should come to light," suggested Milsom.

"I suppose so, sir, but from our point of view it is deplorable. Now sir, if you'll have a look through these…"

Indeed it was a collection. Every criminal type was represented—the brutal bully, the poor, weak youth, the pseudo man-about-town—none was missing. Milsom looked carefully at them all and shook his head. The sergeant was closing the book when his visitor uttered an exclamation.

"No, the man I'm looking for isn't there, but this bloke here was sitting beside him."

Sergeant Thoms leaned over to look. "Oh! That fellow," he said to Richardson, "is Bertram Townsend, alias Frank Wills. He always works in couples with Robert Burton, but Burton is fly and has never yet been convicted: that's why his photograph isn't here. But Burton's time will come," he concluded philosophically. "We must give him time."

"Do you think that the name of the man whose photograph I was looking for is Burton?"

"Quite probably it is."

"Isn't there some way in which one can get a sight of him?"

"Do you think," asked Richardson, "that there would be any chance of my gaining admission to that club of yours off Piccadilly Circus? Do you know how to wangle an entry?"

"I think that I could pull the strings for myself with my waiter friend at the bottom of the stairs, but I shouldn't like to spoil my chances by attempting to smuggle you in: you are too well known. I'm afraid that you'll have to work by deputy."

"Well, I'm not going to detain you any longer now; I must think things out. But I'll ring you up at your office later in the day."

Milsom groaned tragically. "With fresh orders, I suppose. I only hope that they lead somewhere."

Chapter Twenty

ON LEAVING headquarters, Richardson drove Milsom at his request to the office where he spent his time in reading thrillers for publication, or more often for return to their authors. Before they parted, Richardson put one question to him.

"Have you ever heard of a bridge club called the Worthing, a place where the stakes are high?"

"You mean a cock-and-hen club. I've heard of it, but it's a most respectable place. You're surely not thinking of raiding it."

"Good God, no. I asked because a certain lady, the owner of one of those bags we found in the bungalow, frequents it, or did frequent it until her husband put the shutters up against her."

Milsom pulled out his notebook. "Give me the lady's name. I happen to know someone who is a member of that club and may know something about her."

"The name is Mrs Esther. She is a well-groomed young lady of rather striking looks; she lives at 9 Parkside Mansions. I want to know something about her friends at the club, if you've any means of finding out for me."

"I can't promise to get you the information within the next twenty-four hours, if you mean that, because I may not run across my acquaintance for a day or two, and it's not the sort of question one could well ask over the telephone."

Richardson's next point of call was at the lawyer's office in Southampton Street. He was at once shown into the senior partner's room. To him he recounted the adventures of Otway and Maddox at Liverpool, and told him that the men were actually on their way down to London in custody.

"But this is serious, Mr Richardson," said Jackson: "an attempt to escape the jurisdiction."

"In order to regularize the police action I was wondering whether you would have time to obtain a warrant from the Bow Street magistrate."

Jackson looked at the clock and rang his bell. His managing clerk made his appearance. To him the circumstances were explained.

"I will get out an information at once and send a clerk with it to Bow Street. Let me see. Who is sitting today? Mr Ramsbotham. He is pretty quick in the uptake and will grant us a warrant at once when the circumstances are explained to him."

Richardson was not ill-pleased with the way in which things were now moving. Otway and Maddox had been disposed of; if necessary the weakling, Grant, could be frightened into revealing what he knew against the two by being served with a summons for aiding and abetting the fraud, but the little he could tell would not be of much use. The person who held the key to the whole mystery was Casey. The most careful search of the bungalow and enquiries at the bank had failed to produce any compromising document which Casey and Stella Pomeroy had been using as material for blackmail, therefore it was evident that Casey must be holding it. Two interviews with him had been abortive, and a third failure was not to be thought of. There was not at present any evidence on which he could lawfully be searched. He had not been guilty of a felony and could not be arrested. How was he to be dealt with? Not by any short cut. And at this moment the car drew up at Ealing Police Station. Evidently Richardson was anxiously expected, for he saw D.D. Inspector Aitkin at the top of the stairs.

"I'm glad you've come, sir. There's been an accident to a friend of ours this morning—a motor accident. Casey has been run over by a big car on his way to the station, and he's been taken to hospital."

"The Cottage Hospital here?"

"Yes sir. We haven't yet had the report of the house surgeon, but I understand that there were no bones broken."

"Were there any witnesses to the accident?"

"Yes sir, there were five. We've taken rough statements from them. Mr Bruce, a commission agent, who was walking with Casey, tells a rather strange story. He's downstairs now, and I think you might like to see him."

"Very well, have him up."

Mr Bruce proved to be a man of about thirty-five. He was still suffering from the effects of the recent accident in which he himself had also been involved.

"Come in, Mr Bruce," said Richardson; "come in and sit down. I'm sorry to hear about your accident this morning."

"Oh, I wasn't much hurt, and I shall be quite all right in another half-hour. It was Casey that took the shock."

"How did it happen?"

"Well, I'll tell you, and I hope that you'll find the driver of that car and make it hot for him. It was the most bare-faced thing I've ever seen. Mr Casey and I were walking along almost in the gutter when we heard a car coming up behind. By instinct we fell into single file, with me in front and Casey behind. We didn't mount the curb because it was pleasanter walking in the road, but you know what those roads are—twenty feet wide at the very least, and the driver had the whole width to himself. It was quite clear. Well, the first thing I knew was Casey barging into me and knocking me down onto the path. A car had caught him with its mudguard somewhere about the waist and knocked him over like a ninepin."

"Can you give me a description of the car?"

"I can't give you its number, if that's what you mean. The driver had taken good care of that, but it was a biggish touring car painted black, and there was no one in it but the driver."

"Surely you could have taken its number."

"No, that's the funny part of it. There was a big rug over the back; it didn't look as if it had been fixed there on purpose, but I'm quite satisfied that it was. It might have looked to most people as if the wind had caught it and brought it down obliquely so that its corner obscured the number of the car."

"Do you think the driver knew that he had hit Mr Casey?"

"Knew! How could he help knowing? He must have seen Casey barge into me and send me flying onto the path. He must have been one of those road hogs you hear of, who think that the road belongs to them and that cyclists and pedestrians have no right to live. He couldn't have been drunk at that hour in the morning; he couldn't have left the crown of the road except to run into us, because there was no other vehicle to be seen."

"Can you give a description of the driver?"

"Only that he was a youngish man with a slight moustache."

"But surely with the wind the car was making in its passage, the rug would have been flapping."

"I was coming to that. The rug wasn't flapping, because it had been tied down to the petrol tank."

"Have we got this statement down?" asked Richardson of Aitkin.

"Yes sir, in rough; they're typing it out now for Mr Bruce's signature. Ah, here it is."

The youngest patrol bustled in with the typed statement. Mr Bruce read it over and signed it.

"Now, get out an SOS message to all the A.A. scouts in the neighbourhood, asking whether a car of this description has been observed and stopped for having its rear number obscured."

"Very good, sir, but I'm afraid that if it was done purposely, as Mr Bruce thinks, there's not much hope. The driver would seek a lonely stretch of road to cut loose the rug and leave the number unobscured."

"Very well, Mr Bruce, we will endeavour to trace the driver. Would you like someone to take you home?"

"Oh no, thanks. I'm quite fit to go by myself now, but I shan't go up to town until the afternoon. I've put my address in my statement. If you should manage to trace that driver, I hope you'll let me know."

"Certainly. We shall want your evidence for prosecuting him."

Left to themselves, Richardson discussed the accident with Aitkin.

"What about your other four witnesses? Do they corroborate Mr Bruce's statement?"

"Yes, they do—an errand boy in particular, who says that it was the most deliberate thing he had ever seen."

"You see how this evidence fits in with our theory. Assuming that Casey is continuing to blackmail certain persons, they are taking the same rough and ready method with him as they did with his confederate, Stella Pomeroy. We seem likely to have another case of murder on our hands. It was the same hour in the morning that Stella Pomeroy met her death."

"It would be no loss if they got Casey," muttered Aitkin. "It's a pity we can't search his room while he's in hospital."

"Yes, but there would be a most unholy outcry if we did. Remember, Casey is a journalist on the staff of one of these sensational newspapers; we should have questions asked in the House of Commons. And then there are always some of our judges who play to the gallery and trounce the police for accepting confessions from prisoners, leaving the public with the impression that the little accident which brings a man into the dock is the kind of thing that might happen to anybody, and that the real enemies of society are the police. No, we must resign ourselves to the fact that the difficulties put in the way of the police in cases of blackmail are practically insuperable, unless, of course, the victim can be induced to come forward and prosecute. I'm hoping to get a little more evidence which will induce that Mrs Esther to come forward and make a clean breast of it."

"You don't think that Casey would be in the mood for telling a little bit of the truth after his accident?"

"I daresay that he's a bit scared if he realizes that it wasn't an accident, but he would have to make very damning admissions if he told the whole truth: that's the difficulty."

"I wonder who the blighter is that's taking his revenge in this way? Do you suppose that he himself has been blackmailed?"

"Not necessarily. I remember a case—it was one of Chief Inspector Foster's—in which a woman was being blackmailed, and her brother took up the cudgels on her behalf. I use the word cudgels advisedly, because he broke two over the man's head before he had done with him. He was prosecuted for assault, but the Bench, when they heard his defence, only fined him five pounds for a common assault, and he told Foster that he had had good value for his money. I'd like to have Casey's impression of the accident. How would it be to ring up the hospital and ask how he is and whether he would be fit to be seen by a police officer?"

"Yes, but it would be better to say a visitor: he would certainly refuse to be interviewed by one of us. Shall I make the call?"

"Please do."

The news from the hospital was reassuring. The patient had sustained bruises and was rather severely shaken, but he would be discharged on the following morning and he was quite fit to receive a visitor.

"I'll run up there at once," said Richardson.

He found Casey, a rather deflated Casey, in bed in an open ward. At first he seemed disinclined to make any statement to his visitor, but when he understood that the object of the visit was to discover the identity of the motorist, he was quite ready to talk.

"He was a damned careless driver, that man. He had the whole road open to him. He must have let go of the wheel to swerve as he did right down on us instead of keeping to the crown of the road."

"There are a lot of bad drivers on the road," said Richardson, "but hasn't it occurred to you"—he lowered his voice mysteriously—"that it was a deliberate attempt on your life by someone who has a grudge against you?

The pallor that overspread the patient's face made Richardson uneasy as to whether he had not gone too far, but he soon recovered himself.

"You have a lot of imagination for a police officer, haven't you?"

"I don't think so. There have been a number of cases lately which were put down as accidents, but which were really deliberate attempts at murder. Are you one of those lucky men who have no enemies?"

"I suppose that everyone in the world has enemies."

"We have been putting two and two together, and we can't ignore the fact that your associate, Stella Pomeroy, met a violent death at precisely the same hour as this attempt was made upon your life."

"Well then, isn't it up to you to take your coats off and catch this murderous scoundrel? A daylight murder that can't be solved doesn't redound to the credit of the police, I should think."

"The police can't get on without the loyal assistance of the public. I want you to tell me truthfully why anyone should want you out of the way."

"I've told you that your imagination runs away with you. Isn't it up to you to find the driver of that car, a man who has the effrontery to drive through this settlement and deliberately run someone down—for you suggest that it was done deliberately."

"I do, for the very good reason that he had obscured his rear number plate by tying a rug over it. Steps have already been taken with the A.A. scouts, but so far without result."

"I think you're overstaying the time allowed to visitors, Mr Richardson."

"Don't worry about that, Mr Casey: I'm going; but I'd like you to remember one last word. The police are strong to protect worthy citizens, but they are also stern in their pursuit of wrongdoers."

He had got nothing out of Casey, but he had not expected anything. All that he had done was to frighten him, and that in itself was something, because with mercurial temperaments like the Irish, fear is a potent solvent. At their next interview he hoped to have the trump card in his own hand and to find the Irishman quite communicative.

On his return to the office he found a note on the inspector's table saying that a Mr Milsom desired him to ring him up: he had something to communicate. He made the call, and Milsom's voice asked whether it was Superintendent Richardson speaking.

Reassured on this point he said, "I've rung up to tell you that luck has been on my side. I've been in communication with the person who frequents that club we were talking of, and we are going to meet."

"How soon are you going to see him?"

"Good Lord! It isn't a he; it's a she. She's coming to lunch with me in an hour's time, so you can come to my office about four o'clock and hear all I have gleaned for you."

"Very good, you can expect me at four."

Chapter Twenty-One

AT FOUR O'CLOCK Richardson found Jim Milsom impatiently waiting for him.

"I've just left my little lady, after a very instructive conversation," he said. "Does the name Burton convey anything to you? Robert Burton?"

"Yes, he was the man who works with Townsend alias Wills and hasn't yet been convicted. You remember what Sergeant Thoms of the crime index said about him."

"And we thought that Robert Burton might be the man who was sitting beside Townsend alias Wills in that gambling club and who was making signs to Otway."

"Yes; well..."

"Well, Robert Burton is a friend of your Mrs Esther. The world's small, isn't it?"

"Yes. That's important, because Burton himself is believed to get his living by blackmail."

"Well now, listen to what I've managed to pick up about this Mrs Esther. When she contrives to escape from her censorious husband she enjoys a flutter at high stakes. A little while ago she had a run of bad luck and had to deal out IOU's buttered with charming smiles to the winners, but as the days passed the charming smiles ceased to charm and something had to be done about it. Suddenly she became affluent and paid off her losses. The general opinion was that her husband had unbuttoned and paid up for her, because since then she has become a changed woman. Some have even gone so far as to hint that she will soon be seen decked in the uniform of a Salvation Army lass."

"I suppose that the winners became a little pressing."

"Yes; in that kind of club the rule is pretty strict that gambling debts must be paid on pain of the lumber receiving an intimation from the secretary that her membership hangs in the balance."

"And so she was obliged to find the money somehow."

"And she did."

"And the man Burton, what about him?"

"Ah, that was another thing that brought her into bad odour in the club. Though he's a member, more or less on sufferance, no one likes him. That's all I was able to find out, because my little friend doesn't know the Esther woman intimately; they're on bowing and smiling terms only. Now, what's to be my next job?"

"Well, if it's not asking too much of you, I should like you to go once more to that gambling hell and see whether Burton and the man whose photograph you saw this morning are together again; they may have been merely chance neighbours on the last occasion."

"And they may only chance to go there once in a blue moon. Is this to be part of my daily round in my devotion to the cause of justice?"

"Bear with me for a day or two, when I hope to get the case completed."

And Milsom, who knew his friend, let him go without further questioning.

Richardson was anxious to have an interview with Sergeant Hammett, who had taken on the duty of gleaning information about the tenant of 9 Parkside Mansions. It was worth while walking in that direction after sending his driver to park on the other side of the Serpentine Bridge. Luck favoured him. He ran into Hammett, who was gazing into the window of a bookshop near the Albert Gate.

"Take a turn in the park with me. I want to hear how you have been getting on."

"I haven't done so badly, sir. I've made the acquaintance of Mrs Esther's maid who takes the dog out. She's a forthcoming little woman, and from passing the time of day we've got on to personal matters."

"You might give me the gist of the information you've gathered."

"I've gathered, sir, that Mrs Esther is very unhappy and has gone all to pieces these last few days."

"Why?"

"The maid can't make out why. Her husband is away and is expected back in a day or two, but this doesn't account for her unhappiness, because she is very fond of him."

"Then it's not a case of another man?"

"Oh no, sir; the maid gives her a very good character on that score. I suggested that she had card debts, and the maid agreed with me that that might have been the case a week or two ago, because she had left lots of bills unpaid and even the maid's wages, but suddenly she became quite flush with money and paid up everything. The maid didn't know where she had got the money from to do it, and I said perhaps she had pawned something. The young woman said, 'Well, I thought that too, but I have charge of all her jewellery—it's worth millions—and there's nothing missing, so it couldn't be that.'"

"Did you ask whether she had any male visitors?"

"I did, sir, but she said that there were only one or two, and none that called frequent."

"I think you've done very well, Sergeant. You can knock off observation now. I'll let you know if I want you to do any more."

An idea had crossed Richardson's mind. He felt that he could follow it up better alone than through any of his subordinates. It entailed a tour of jewellers' shops, but we would shorten the quest by beginning with the most likely. He argued that in the transaction he suspected, Mrs Esther would not have been likely to go to any of the jewellers in the West End of London. She would have gone to some firm in North or South London, where she could not personally be known. For one man alone it was going to be a formidable enquiry, but from his knowledge of those in the trade he thought he could shorten it.

At Marsham's, where he was a familiar figure from other days, he drew blank. Mr Marsham welcomed him.

"It's not often we see you now, Superintendent Richardson. Indeed, I don't think that I've had the opportunity of congratulating you on your promotion. What can I do for you today?"

"I want to ask you confidentially whether you have lately undertaken to make a copy in imitation of any article of jewellery brought by a lady, and whether you purchased the real jewels?"

Mr Marsham sniggered. "It's not quite so unusual a transaction as many people think. I won't say that I haven't done such a thing, but not lately."

Richardson had undertaken to visit the most likely of the firms, but he drew blank at two more on his list. At the fourth shop he gained heart again. The proprietor, so far as he knew him, was an honest man, half jeweller, half pawnbroker, in North London.

He invited him into a little room at the back of the shop after calling an assistant to take charge. Richardson put his question to him. The man grinned.

"You know, Mr Richardson, when I see you come into the shop cold shivers run down my back, but I've nothing to fear this time, because the transaction you mention is a perfectly legal one. I took steps to see that everything was in order before I touched the business. A lady, who gave me her name and address in confidence and allowed me to call upon her at her home, commissioned me to do the very thing that you mention."

"Did the lady come to you alone?"

"No; I'll tell you how the business came to me. A gentleman called and proposed the business of copying a genuine pearl necklace of great intrinsic value in cultured pearls. I said that I could do it. Then he asked me whether, if I was satisfied with the value of the genuine pearls, I would purchase them. This was quite an unexpected proposal. I said that I would have to see the owner and satisfy myself that the transaction was an honest one. I said that I did not impugn his good faith in any way, but that that was a rule of the house. He assured me that everything was in order, and if I would guarantee to undertake the business he would give me the lady's name and address and I could call upon her."

"I think I can give you both the name and address without asking you to violate the lady's confidence. It was Mrs Esther of 9 Parkside Mansions."

Plainly the jeweller was startled. "I don't know how you gentlemen at the Yard get to know these things. I am quite sure that you didn't get that information from Mrs Esther herself."

Richardson smiled. "It is by the very simple process that we all learn at school: it's called putting two and two together. Did the gentleman who called on you give you his name?"

"No, but I can give you a fairly accurate description of him. He was tall and slim and very well dressed, with a slight—very slight—cast in one eye. I think in the left eye."

"Did he strike you as a man in whom you would have confidence?"

The jeweller hesitated a moment. "Well, he was dressed like a gentleman, and he spoke like one. I can't say that he impressed me as a man—well, as a man that I would trust with the care of my stock, without further enquiry. In fact I must confess that I wouldn't have undertaken the business at all if I had not seen Mrs Esther personally and satisfied myself that she was the lawful owner of the pearls. One has to be so careful in these days. I got the name of her banker as a reference."

"What bank was it?"

"The National."

"And you did complete the transaction?"

"Yes sir, I did, but as the pearls were of such value I had to get friends in the trade to share the transaction with me. There was one point that worried me a bit. The lady declined to accept a cheque in payment, but insisted upon being paid in bank notes."

"Of what denomination?"

"Well, as far as I remember, in fifties and twenties." Richardson left the jeweller, well satisfied with the result of his enquiry. If Mrs Esther had changed any of these notes for treasury notes with which to pay Stella Pomeroy, she would have had to sign her name on the back. Here was another job for Sergeant Hammett. He rang him up at Ealing Police Station.

"There is one question that I forgot to ask you," he said, when he had Hammett on the line. "Did you find out at what shops that lady is accustomed to deal?"

"Yes sir, I did. She does nearly all her shopping at Harringtons."

"Well, I want you to go tomorrow morning to Harringtons and find out whether she has changed any big notes for treasury notes. If you draw blank there I will call on her bankers myself, but I want to avoid doing that if I can."

"Very good, sir. I know the cashier at Harringtons." Richardson changed the telephone number to that of Jim Milsom's flat.

"Hallo!" exclaimed an impatient voice. "Oh, it's you, Superintendent. What's the new trouble?"

"If you haven't any other engagement this evening I'd be very grateful if you could look in at that place."

"And poison myself with the scent of Balkan humanity. I gather that you're hot on the scent, or you wouldn't dare ring me up again so soon."

"I've got some new dope for you. The gentleman in question has a very slight cast in one of his eyes."

"Poor devil! I wonder he hasn't taken to honest courses instead of risking recognition by that obvious defect. I suppose the truth is, that when you get your nose to the ground on a hot scent you don't want any sleep and so you keep me from my virtuous pillow for company. Very well, I'll sacrifice myself once more, and if you'll come round to my flat at half-past nine, I'll tell you about your friend and stand you a spot of supper into the bargain."

"I think I told you that these people are like ordinary criminals in that they do things in the same way and at approximately the same hour. You were last at that sink of iniquity at eight o'clock or thereabouts. They'll probably be found there each evening at the same hour."

"Right! I'm starting off now, and I'll expect you at half-past nine."

Richardson put in the time by writing up his notes on Mrs Esther, who was becoming so important a factor in the case. At nine-thirty precisely he was rapping at his friend's door. Milsom had returned; his tone was portentous.

"Come in, my friend, and let me unburden myself. Your knowledge of the psychology of these Johnnies is startling. What beats me is why they haven't more imagination. Why frequent the same gambling hell at the same hour night after night? It must be so deadly dull, and they stretch themselves out on the operating table for you police quite oblivious of the danger they are running."

"It all depends on whether they guess that they're being followed. When they are put on the alert you'd be surprised at the variety of artifices that they have up their sleeves. I gather from your buoyancy of manner that you found our two friends in the same place as on the last occasion when you saw them."

"Yes—sitting on the self-same chairs, I could bet."

"After seeing them for the second time what is your opinion? Are they friends or just casual neighbours?"

"Friends; I'd stake my life on that. And what's more, I'd stake my life on the other man being the one I spotted in the photograph album of Sergeant Thoms— Bertram Townsend alias Frank Wills."

"And as Thoms told us, Townsend always works with Burton, and Burton, I find out, has been doing what I think are shady transactions with Mrs Esther. A jeweller I have seen this evening gave me the description of a man who, I think, is Burton: tall and slim, very well dressed, with a slight—very slight—cast in one eye."

"That's the blighter to the life, the fellow who was there this evening with Townsend."

"And in some way which I have not yet got to the bottom of, Townsend and Burton are mixed up with that fellow Otway."

"Yes, of course; I saw them make signals to one another."

"More than that, they've sent Grant down to get hold of Mrs Esther's bag on the excuse of wanting a memento of his dead sister."

"I'm glad that I haven't got you on my heels. I should never sleep soundly again if I had. You must be nearing the end of the puzzle."

"We're getting on," said Richardson, "but we've several bad patches to cross before we get home on the murder."

"I refuse to attempt to cross any bad patch until I've fed. Let me ring the bell."

A waiter appeared in obedience to the summons, and Milsom gave the order with a look of enquiry at his guest at every dish on the menu.

As soon as the first pangs of hunger were assuaged, Richardson related the results of his tour round the jewellers' and his discoveries about the proceedings of Mrs Esther.

"You see, this wretched woman, by letting Burton into her confidence, has delivered herself into the hands of the gang."

"Do you think that murdered woman was one of the gang?"

"Not the Burton gang. I think that she came into it by accident—the accident that she stole Mrs Esther's bag with something compromising in it."

"What?"

"Probably we shall find that it was nothing more than the bill of the jeweller for having substituted cultured pearls for real ones."

"So this poor Mrs Esther is up to her neck in a sea of troubles. These ruffians are blackmailing her with the jeweller's receipt by threatening to show it to her husband. Then another happy home will be broken up, for her husband will never forgive her. Jewels are the apple of his eye. He inherited the passion from a long line of Jerusalem ancestors."

"I'm going to try and squeeze a confession out of her in her own interests, poor wretched woman. Her husband, I learn, is away. I'll get as much as I can settled before he comes back."

"Well, more power to your elbow. Don't let my telephone number slip your memory."

Chapter Twenty-Two

RICHARDSON was in the superintendent's office at New Scotland Yard the following morning, when his telephone bell rang. It was a message from Sergeant Hammett to say that he was speaking from a call office. He had just returned from Harringtons, where he had verified the fact that Mrs Esther had changed two notes of large denomination for bundles of treasury notes.

This report was sufficient to warrant Richardson's calling on Mrs Esther, and he was just putting on his overcoat when the telephone bell rang again.

"I want to speak to Superintendent Richardson," said a man's voice. "I am Principal Warder Parker, speaking from Brixton Prison."

"Superintendent Richardson speaking."

"We have a prisoner here, sir, who has applied to the governor for a private interview with you."

"What's his name?"

"James Maddox, sir."

"A private interview?"

"Yes sir. That means in sight but out of hearing of a prison officer, but that does not preclude you from bringing a second police officer with you to act as a witness, because I might tell you confidentially that the prisoner is not a man whose word can be trusted."

Richardson decided that Brixton Prison should be his first port of call in order to give time to Mrs Esther to be up and dressed: a lady might object to be called on by a police officer at half-past nine. Huggins was directed to drive to Brixton Prison. He parked the car at the gate, and Richardson asked the gatekeeper to keep an eye on it while he and Huggins were in the visiting room. They had to wait for a few minutes while the prisoner was brought from his cell.

When the warder had brought him to the wire screen and had withdrawn out of earshot, Richardson said,

"I understand from the governor that you wish to see me."

"Yes sir, I do. I've made a fool of myself, and I deserve anything the Court may give me, but I'm not the worst in this business. I was put up to it by another chap, and I think there's dirtier work behind all this that you ought to look into."

"If you like to make a statement I'm ready to take it down."

"Well, I'll begin right at the beginning. Just as Mr Colter died in New Zealand, my brother Ted met with a serious accident out motoring. He was too ill to travel, but he sent for me and gave me all the letters and the will and asked me to take them over to the lawyers in England. Well, I started, but when I got down to Wellington I got a telegram to say that poor Ted was dead. I'd got my ticket by then, and so I came just the same. We were one day out when I ran across Otway in the smoking room. He got very friendly, and I told him all about my brother's death and the legacy. Well, then he got me playing cards, and it was uncanny the way that man had all the luck. One night he kept plying me with drinks until I didn't know where I was or what I was doing, and the next morning he showed me an IOU, signed by me in a very shaky hand, for five thousand pounds. I was knocked all of a heap, but he was very nice about it, and said that there was no hurry and he wouldn't have pressed me at all if it wasn't that he himself was being pressed to pay a gambling debt.

"He used to ask me about my family. I told him that there were seven of us until Ted died, and he said, 'What a pity: you'll have to share the estate with five brothers and sisters.' And then a day or two later he said, 'I've been thinking over your affairs. If you had been your eldest brother you would have inherited the lot. Why shouldn't you impersonate your brother Ted when you see the lawyers in England? They won't know the difference, and you'll get the lot. Mr Colter had quite a big fortune, and you can be generous to your brothers and sisters.'"

"But Stella Pomeroy knew your brother Ted," said Richardson.

"Yes, and that was the snag, but that devil had an idea for getting over that. There was a codicil to the will about founding an agricultural college for emigrants. He said that he could cut that off in such a way that no one could spot it; that I ought to go straight to Stella Pomeroy with the will and tell her that if she'd agree to say that I was Ted we'd cut that off and share the whole lot between us. As luck would have it, when I got to the bungalow I found that she was dead, so it all seemed plain sailing."

"What about her brother?"

"Well, I met him at the funeral and he didn't seem to know that I wasn't Ted, but Otway said we had better keep him under our thumb. It wasn't difficult, because the lawyers unbelted and paid out cash by the week. Otway was a trial all this time. He was clamouring for the five thousand on my IOU, and sometimes he was quite threatening about it."

"Why did you send Grant down to the bungalow to get a lady's black handbag mounted in gold?"

"I didn't send him: it was Otway; and that's what I was coming to. There's something dirty behind that business of the bag. I don't know what it is: it's for you to find out; but Otway's got some shady friends."

"Didn't he tell you why he wanted the bag?"

"Oh, he told me a cock-and-bull story about a friend of his who was supposed to have given it to Stella Pomeroy and was afraid that his wife might get to hear of it."

"Did he introduce you to a man named Burton?"

"Yes. He told me that they had met in New Zealand when Burton was on a trip round the world. Burton said, 'Are you the man who was co-heir with Stella Pomeroy?' I said, 'Yes, but how did you know?' 'Oh,' he said, 'it was all in the papers—how you had gone to her bungalow with the news that she had come into a fortune and found that she had been foully murdered half an hour before your arrival. They made quite a song and dance of it.'"

"Well, this ought to be a lesson to you: you can't get away with frauds of this kind in England."

"Of course if I told you that I don't care two pence about becoming a rich man you wouldn't believe me, but that's the fact, and as long as I don't have to pay Otway his five thousand I don't care. The funny thing is that when we came out of chapel this morning I found myself walking just in front of him. He whispered, 'A still tongue, remember, makes a wise head.' I wonder what he'd think if he knew what I've been telling you this last twenty minutes?"

Richardson made a sign to the warder that the interview was at an end. The prisoner saw the signal and said, "Mind you, I haven't been telling you this with the idea of doing myself a bit of good. It was because I feel sure that there's a crime more serious than mine behind that black bag, and I think that you ought to know it."

"Very well, I won't forget it."

He and Huggins returned to the car and drove to Parkside Mansions, where Richardson learned that Mrs Esther had not yet gone out. He was whisked up in the lift to the third floor and shown into the sitting room to wait while the maid carried his card to her mistress. He was kept waiting an unconscionable time, and when Mrs Esther did make her appearance he saw that the cause of the delay was the extra coating of rouge she had administered to her cheeks to conceal her pallor.

She had screwed up her courage to the point of opening the attack.

"If you've come to worry me again about that wretched bag I shall write to headquarters to complain about you."

Richardson adopted his suavest manner. "I shouldn't have ventured to call again about that bag if it hadn't been for your own mistake in describing it."

"My mistake?" she exclaimed indignantly.

"Yes, madam. At the stores where you complained of having lost it you described it as being mounted in gold; to me you said that it had ivory mountings."

"My bag has ivory mountings. I can show it to you."

"I have no doubt that you can show me a bag with ivory mountings, but the bag that you lost and that we have recovered for you has gold mountings."

The look of a hunted animal came into her eyes. "Supposing that it was my bag, why are you interested in it?"

His manner changed. He was grave as he said, "Mrs Esther, I must impress upon you that behind the loss of your bag lies a very serious crime, and it is out of a desire to protect you from the consequences that I am visiting you this morning. I beg you to tell me the whole truth."

"I'll tell you nothing," she said defiantly.

"Then I must tell you," said Richardson, drawing a bow at a venture. "In that bag was the jeweller's account for exchanging pearls of high value for imitations."

All her bravado deserted her. She licked her dry lips and tried to speak, but her words were unintelligible. Near the window was a cocktail cabinet. Richardson went to it and poured out a glass of brandy, which he brought over to her and induced her to swallow.

"That's better," he said. "Now, Mrs Esther, let me repeat once more that my sole desire is to help and protect you. If you will tell me the whole truth you will never regret it."

"What do you want to know?" she asked.

"When did Stella Pomeroy begin to blackmail you about the contents of your bag? Tell me the whole of your transactions with her as far as you remember them."

"Well, to begin at the beginning. I had my bag stolen in the hat department at a big store. I made a complaint at the office downstairs. A day or two later I received a letter signed 'Stella Pomeroy.'"

"Have you kept the letter?"

"Yes."

"Will you show it to me?"

She rose and went to her writing table and returned with several letters, one of which she handed to him. Richardson frowned as he read it.

DEAR MADAM:

A certain person has come to me with an extraordinary story concerning a handbag, which apparently belongs to you, and claims that the contents of the bag are of great value to you. This person sets the value at £500. I cannot, of course, judge how far this claim is justified, but I am willing to act in your interest as an intermediary if you care to communicate with me saying that you accept my services in that capacity. I think that I am in a position to bring considerable pressure to bear on the person in question in the interests of justice.

Yours faithfully,

STELLA POMEROY.

Richardson thought that he detected Casey's hand in the wording of this letter.

"Did you send any reply to this?"

"I applied to a friend to act for me."

"How could the writer of this letter have guessed that the jeweller's bill would compromise you with your husband?"

Even through the rouge Richardson could see the increased pallor.

"There was a note—an unsigned note—with the bill, saying that my husband would never detect the change."

"You paid this woman two hundred pounds in treasury notes."

"I paid more than that—much more. You can see by these letters how she kept demanding more."

Richardson read through the letters she passed to him. He noticed that they mentioned no sum, but only said that she couldn't get the person who held the bag to relinquish it until the whole demand had been paid.

"Who acted for you as intermediary with this woman, Stella Pomeroy?"

"I can't give you the name; surely you can see that."

"How much did you pay altogether to regain possession of your bag and its contents?"

"Altogether nearly a thousand pounds."

"Why didn't you bring that first letter straight to the police? You might have saved yourself all this extortion."

"I was afraid that it might get round indirectly to my husband—as I suppose it will do now." Her composure gave way, and she burst into tears.

Richardson waited until the first storm had abated; then he said, "It is too late now for us to talk of what you might have done, but I assure you that this is the moment for telling everything and keeping nothing back. This woman is dead."

"I know: I saw it in the papers."

"So you haven't paid anything since her death?"

"No, but it is still being demanded."

"By a man named Casey?"

"Yes. How much do you know? If you know everything, why do you torture me with these questions?"

"Because in my chain of evidence there are one or two links missing, and I think you can supply them." He paused a moment and then continued gravely, "That hush money that you paid—did you pay it through Mr Burton?"

"Oh, my God! You have no missing links for me to supply. You've found it all out."

"When are you to see Burton again?"

"Not today, thank God; not until tomorrow evening."

"Then you have two days respite, unless, of course, he comes a day earlier than he arranged."

"He never does that. He won't come unless it gets round to him that Scotland Yard are acting."

"He won't know that yet—not until it acts to some purpose as far as he's concerned."

"I suppose all the newspapers will come out with big headlines about what I've done."

"I don't think you need be afraid of that. Your name will be kept out of this; it won't appear in any newspaper. Now I want you to allow me to keep these letters, and if you have one from the man Casey please give it to me."

"This is his." She handed him the last of the letters she was holding.

DEAR MADAM [it ran]:

Before her death Mrs Stella Pomeroy banded over to me the task of recovering the documents in which you are interested. I am endeavouring to negotiate on your behalf but the transaction is expensive and the person demands uncompromisingly another £200.

Yours faithfully,

DENNIS CASEY.

With the letters safely folded in his pocket, Richardson went round to the Home Office to apply to the prison commissioners for an order to see the prisoner Otway in Brixton Prison. He promised himself the diversion of another interview later in the day with Dennis Casey.

He obtained the order for Brixton Prison almost immediately, but he decided to postpone the interview until after the dinner hour.

Chapter Twenty-Three

THE WARDERS at Brixton Prison were streaming back from their quarters to the main gate when Richardson's car arrived. They looked a smart and hefty lot as they went in to draw their keys from the gatekeeper. Richardson reflected that but for the grace of God he might have been pursuing this monotonous round of duty without any break in it from one end of the year to the other. When the inner gate had clanged to behind the warders and the men who had been on duty during the dinner hour had delivered up their keys and gone out to consume their belated meal, he presented his visiting order and, after a few minutes delay, Otway was conducted to the visiting room. Richardson congratulated himself that he had arrived in advance of the regular visiting hours, when each visitor vied with his neighbour in shouting him down.

Otway appeared to be in a subdued frame of mind, the frame of mind that makes the most obstinate man plastic. Richardson opened the conversation.

"I've been wondering why a man of your intelligence and education should have got Maddox to personate his brother—the fraud was bound to be found out."

"I've been wondering why I should be accused of having put Maddox up to it. I never went near the lawyers; I made no statements; I got no money out of them—"

"Not directly, I know, but you got money through Maddox and shared in the fraud. But I didn't come to discuss that kind of thing with you. I came to see whether you are disposed now to tell us who was at the bottom of the business of sending Arthur Grant down to his sister's bungalow to get one of her handbags."

"I'm not responsible for the weak sentiment of Arthur Grant."

"It wasn't sentiment that induced Arthur Grant to go down. As you know very well it was the promise of money, and you know who the promise came from."

"How should I know?"

"Because it came through you. Let me help your memory a little. The offer came from Mr Burton, whoever was providing the money."

"Then if you knew that why do you come to see me?"

"Because we may want your evidence."

"And if I told the truth about it, would the authorities withdraw the prosecution against me?"

"That is a question I can't answer, but if you tell the truth no doubt it will be considered in the proper quarter."

"Well, what I'm going to tell you doesn't incriminate me in any way, and so you may as well have it."

"When did you first make Burton's acquaintance?"

"It was in New Zealand a year ago."

"Was your object in coming to England to renew your acquaintance with him?"

"Partly. He had half promised to find me a job over here."

"You knew where to find him in London?"

"I did. He told me where to write to."

"Was it pure coincidence that you were interested in Maddox and that Burton was interested in Stella Pomeroy?"

"You seem to know quite a lot. I wonder that you thought it worth while to come down and pump me."

"Because if you like to open up and come out with the whole truth it will make my work lighter."

"Well, I called on Burton a day or two after I arrived in London and told him that I was staying at the Palace Hotel with a man called Maddox. He asked if it was the Maddox whose name had been in the papers in connection with the bungalow murder. I said that he was the same man."

"And you pointed Maddox out to him at that gambling club off Piccadilly Circus."

"You are right again, Superintendent; I did."

"Didn't he want to be introduced to Maddox?"

"No; on the contrary, that was just what he did not wish."

"I see. He thought it would be safer to work through you. Did he tell you why he wanted that lady's handbag? Of course I have heard the little fairy tale about the man who had given it to Stella Pomeroy and was afraid that his wife might get to hear of it. That was food enough for Arthur Grant, but I'm sure that it wouldn't have satisfied you."

Otway grinned. "As a matter of fact that little tale was my own invention, and it worked beautifully with Grant."

"But the real purpose was to get it back for the owner, who was willing to pay a high price for its recovery. Did Burton tell you that?"

'Yes."

"Did he tell you that he had already made an unsuccessful attempt to get it back by burgling the bungalow?"

"He hinted as much."

"Has Burton a high-powered motorcar?"

"He doesn't own one, but he hires when he requires one."

"From what garage?"

"Hosking's in Oxford Street."

"You can't think of anything else that Burton told you in connection with the bungalow and that bag?"

"If I did know anything more I should tell you in order to gain favour." Otway smiled sarcastically. "I can assure you, Superintendent, that I value my own skin so highly that it would give me no qualms to round on a pal, but I know nothing else against Burton. He is too close and too clever to give anything away, even if he wants one to work with him."

Richardson knew enough of this type of man to know that he was speaking the truth and had no further information to give that would be helpful, but he had verified all his own surmises and found them correct.

"Of course," he said, "I can make you no promises, because your fate doesn't rest with the police, but I'll see that what you've told me is brought to the notice of the proper authority. Don't build too highly on what I may be able to do for you. Good-bye."

There was now Casey to see, and he had first to find out whether he had left the Cottage Hospital. A ring on the telephone from a call office was enough to settle that question: Casey had left and had gone home. Richardson drove back to Ealing and stopped the car at the house of Mrs Coxon. He sent a message upstairs by the landlady, inviting Casey to come down and speak to him. After some delay the Irishman made his appearance at the front door.

"I'm sorry to disturb a man recovering from an accident, but I have one or two more questions to ask you, and if you'll take a turn in the car with me I'll bring you back to this door."

"You seem very fond of my society lately, Superintendent."

"It's quite natural, as I think you will admit when you hear what I have to say. Jump in, and we'll go for a drive, unless you would prefer to see me in the house."

"We couldn't talk there for brats. I suppose you don't mean to kidnap me and starve me in an underground cellar as they do in the films."

"No, in this country the oubliette is a thing of the past. It must have had its uses, though."

Casey climbed painfully into the car.

"Drive slowly," said Richardson to Huggins. "In our former interviews, Mr Casey, you have always declined to let me into your confidence. This did not prevent me from gathering certain information bearing upon you."

Whether it was the effect of his accident, or whether Richardson's tone of quiet confidence impressed him, Casey lost his usual truculence.

"What information have you gathered?" he asked wearily.

"For one thing, I have come into possession of a letter written by you."

"You have lately found more than one letter written by me. I suppose this was addressed to Stella Pomeroy."

"No. This was addressed to a Mrs Esther."

"Well?"

"You are aware that blackmail is very heavily punished by the courts in these days."

"When it's proved. There was no blackmail in my letter."

"The court will be the best judge of that."

"Oh, that needn't worry you. I have a very sound defence. It might interest you to hear it."

"It would, very much."

Casey cleared his throat mockingly. "Well, gentlemen of the jury. The police having embarked on a futile line of investigation into the murder of Stella Pomeroy, I decided that it was in the public interest that I should conduct an enquiry of my own."

"Being in possession of the fact that Stella Pomeroy was being paid sums of money by blackmail. Didn't it strike you that it was your duty to put these facts into the possession of the police?"

"What, and blacken a dead woman's memory? Besides, I knew enough of the British police to be sure that they would muddle it."

"One of the letters addressed by you to Stella Pomeroy speaks of 'the dangerous game that we are playing.' She handed certain documents over to you for safe keeping, and you knew for what purpose she was using them."

"Gentlemen of the jury—" Casey resumed the lecturer's voice. "You may feel sure that I had but one motive in taking charge of those papers—to prevent them from being used any more for a criminal purpose."

"Well, now that your mission has been fulfilled, you will, of course, hand the papers over to me."

"Not quite so fast, my dear Superintendent. You forget that I am a journalist and that it would be quite a scoop for my paper to be able to announce that where the Metropolitan Police failed, our representative had taken up the investigation and carried it to a successful conclusion."

"You must be a credit to your profession, Mr Casey. Your defence is excellent journalism, but that is all that can be said for it. I may tell you that the papers we are speaking of would be practically the last link in the chain of evidence against the murderer of Mrs Pomeroy. As that, on your own showing, is what you have been working for, I'm sure you will welcome this opportunity for handing them to me. I can assure you that your newspaper will have all the scoop that it wants—if you still wish it—when the murderer is brought to trial."

"You can't be allowed to have all the surprises on your side, my dear Superintendent. Look at this, for example: this is the envelope which Stella Pomeroy handed to me, and, as you can see for yourself, the seal is still unbroken."

Richardson switched on the light in the interior of the car and scrutinized the seal. The envelope had been sealed with the same seal that Inspector Aitkin had found in searching the bungalow—a double E intertwined—which had obviously been in the bag stolen by Stella Pomeroy. Here Casey was speaking the truth. The letter must have been sealed by Stella Pomeroy and handed to him as he said. Richardson realized the cunning displayed by the man sitting beside him.

"I shall open this letter at the police station in the presence of Inspector Aitkin. Do you wish to be present?"

"No, but I'll ask you to take me home. I am not so sure of my legs as I was before my accident."

Richardson directed Huggins to the door of Casey's lodgings and dropped him there.

Returning to the police station he mounted the stairs and entered Aitkin's room flourishing the sealed envelope.

"What have you got there, Superintendent?"

"I don't know until we've opened it. It's a sealed letter from Stella Pomeroy addressed to Casey."

"You mean that he's never read it?"

"No, the dog was too cunning for that; he held this; sealed letter as a proof to clear himself. He was going to pretend that he knew nothing of its contents."

While he was speaking he slit the letter open and pulled out of it three separate, folded papers. One was the jeweller's bill that Mrs Esther was so anxious to recover; the second was the incriminating note that she need have no fear that her husband would ever find out the deception; the third Richardson read aloud.

"Listen to this with both your ears, Aitkin:

"I shall call at your bungalow tomorrow morning, September 13th, at the hour you mention, 8:30. Kindly have the articles ready so that you do not keep me waiting. I shall bring the necessary with me.

"R.B."

"Who on earth is R.B.?" asked Aitkin, mystified.

"They are initials that will be familiar to you before you are much older. They stand for Richard Burton, the man that we've been hunting down since September thirteenth." Richardson proceeded to take the inspector into his confidence about all his movements during the last two days.

"Well, it's the unexpected that happens. When did you first begin to suspect him?"

"As soon as I learned that he was acting as intermediary between Mrs Esther and Stella Pomeroy. He was squeezing Mrs Esther for two thousand pounds and trying to get the papers from Stella Pomeroy for two hundred. I suppose he found her stubborn and so he laid her out, but I'm going off now to see Casey again and get from him a few more details."

"But that won't be enough evidence to arrest Burton for murder."

"No, it won't, but I shan't rest until I've got enough."

He ran down the stairs, jumped into the car and directed Huggins once more to drive to Casey's lodgings. He told Mrs Coxon that he had urgent business with her lodger, and she showed him up to the bed-sitting-room on the first floor, where he found the Irish journalist sitting in an armchair reading a newspaper. He started to his feet.

"Can't a man have a corner to himself in any part of England?"

"I'm sorry to disturb you, Mr Casey, but we can't very well leave things unfinished. I want you to tell me when Mrs Pomeroy handed you that letter—the sealed letter which you gave to me just now."

"On the evening before her death. She met me at the station and asked me to take care of it."

"Did she tell you that someone was to call for it on the following morning?"

"She said the next day, and that she meant to give them a run for their money, or words to that effect."

"Then you knew that a stranger had called on Mrs Pomeroy. Why didn't you tell me that?"

"Because it would have led to a lot of complications and stirred up a lot of dirty water unnecessarily. I told you that I was trying to hunt down the murderer by myself."

"He tried to hunt you down in his car yesterday morning; you had a narrow escape. Have you ever had an interview with this man?"

"Never."

"Nor any correspondence?"

"Never."

"Well, I don't think I shall have to disturb you again tonight, Mr Casey."

"You are welcome to all the help I've given you. By the way, Superintendent, did you discover who committed the burglary at the bungalow the other evening?"

"Yes; Richard Burton, but I shan't call you to identify him, although I know that you were watching his proceedings from a safe distance."

Chapter Twenty-Four

ON LEAVING Ealing Richardson drove to the garage indicated by Otway—Hosking's in Oxford Street. He knew that the evidence he had against Burton was insufficient even to insure his committal for trial, and he was praying that he might light upon something at the garage that would be a strong connecting link in the case.

He found a middle-aged lady installed in the little glass cubbyhole which served as an office. Taking him for a promising-looking customer she removed her glasses and smiled upon him; learning that he was a police officer seeking information against one of her customers, she resumed them and gazed at him with a touch-me-if-you-dare scrutiny.

"I'm sorry to trouble you, madam, but you have a customer, a Mr Burton, who, we understand, occasionally hires cars from you." The lady inclined her head without speaking. "I want you to look up the dates since the beginning of September when he has hired from you."

With a perfunctory movement she turned over the pages of her diary. "He took out a car yesterday morning at eight and returned it at ten."

"And before yesterday?"

She flipped back the pages. "Oh, here, in the evening of Wednesday, from eight-thirty to ten-thirty."

"And before that?"

She flipped back a few more pages.

"Try September thirteenth," suggested Richardson. "Yes, here it is; from 8 A.M. to 10.30 A.M."

"Was it an open car?"

"You'd better ask the foreman about that: he knows what car he gave him better than I do."

The foreman was quite cheerful and explicit. "Know Mr Burton? Of course I do. He's one of our regular customers. Is he going to be pinched for exceeding the speed limit? I know he must go at a pace sometimes. Once he lost the toolbox out of the car with all the tools in it."

Richardson began to revile himself for lack of thoroughness in his investigations. "Was there a hammer among the lost tools?" he asked.

"Yes, and it was my own favourite hammer."

"Had you any means of knowing it from other hammers?"

"Yes, my name's Phillips, and I'd scratched a P on the handle. If I saw it I'd know it from a thousand other hammers."

"When Mr Burton took out that car yesterday did you lend him a rug?"

"Yes. He asked for one because it was such a cold morning, so I lent him one."

Richardson thanked him and directed Huggins to drive him back to Ealing. He dashed upstairs to Aitkin, who was waiting for him.

"Before we do anything else, D.D. Inspector, tell me, where is the hammer with which we thought Stella Pomeroy was killed?"

"I have it here in the safe." Aitkin took it out and land it on the table. "That's the one with Pomeroy's own initial on the handle."

"I believe we've made a mistake here. There are other names beginning with a P. This hammer may have done the murder, but it belongs to a garage foreman named Phillips and was lost by a man named Burton, who hired a car from him."

"Good God!"

"Yes. Burton, having left the hammer on the scene of the crime, was artful enough to lose the toolbox and all its contents."

"But Pomeroy admitted that it was his."

"I don't think Pomeroy was in a state to deny anything that was put to him that morning, but his hammer must be found. Send every available man to move the coal in the bungalow outhouse as early as possible tomorrow morning to see whether they can find it."

"Very good, sir. Are you doing any more tonight?"

"No, but I shall be up early in the morning."

Early as Richardson's arrival in Ealing was on the following morning, the local police were ready for him. They had discovered Pomeroy's hammer buried under one ton of coal. That hammer, too, was marked P, but the letter had been branded more deeply than it had on the hammer found in the ornamental pond.

As soon as he thought that his chief would be in his office, Richardson called on Mr Morden with the two hammers and the correspondence he had collected during his investigation.

Morden listened patiently to his narration of the facts and examined the correspondence.

"You have done well, Mr. Richardson. I think that we now have a watertight case for the director of public prosecutions. I'll mark the papers over to him, and you can take them across by hand, together with such exhibits as are necessary. See that everything is properly labelled before you leave it. Of course if you had sifted the matter of the hammer earlier in the case you might have arrived sooner at the result, but I doubt whether you would have had the same amount of evidence as you have now got."

Richardson went off with his report and exhibits to the barrister in the office of the director of public prosecutions with whom he was wont to deal.

On leaving that office he felt that he owed it to Jim Milsom to pay him an impromptu visit and thank him for all the assistance he had given.

"I feel that it must be some compensation to you, Mr Milsom, to know that we have arrived at a result. It is practically certain now that the murderer of Stella Pomeroy will be brought to trial, and that is largely due to the help you have given me. If you had not spotted the secret undemanding that existed between Otway and that unknown man in the gambling den, we might have taken much longer."

Jim Milsom regarded him with a whimsical eye. "I don't quite remember the formula on these occasions, but I think that historically speaking the sleuths fill their glasses and drink to the common hangman. So here goes."

"Nothing stronger than sherry, thank you, Mr Milsom. Now, to return to the man whose name we now know as Burton: did you notice whether on that evening he left the gambling room some time before your party did?"

"Yes, we hadn't been there long when he left."

"Then he would have had time to break into the bungalow that evening."

"What will be done to Maddox and Otway?"

"I fancy that they'll get off rather lightly, because they will be useful to us as witnesses when Burton is brought to trial. I understand from Mr Jackson that Maddox has not cheated him at present out of more than his own share of Colter's estate would come to. The solicitor can, if he likes, deduct the money when he pays over cash to the legatees."

"The person who interests me in all this," said Milsom, "is that Mrs Esther. Granted that she was a fool, she's had a rotten time, and when her husband comes home she may have a worse time still."

"We shall have to use her, of course, but she will be a mystery woman as far as the newspapers are concerned—a Mrs X who was being blackmailed by Pomeroy. As for her husband, if he gets to know of it he must settle that with his wife."

Richardson had one more helper to thank before he could consider the case as closed as far as he was concerned. This was Ann Pomeroy. With that more pressing business in prospect he declined Jim Milsom's invitation to lunch with him. He hoped to surprise Ann in that little den which opened out of the hall in her uncle's house in the act of taking her coffee after lunch. So he contented himself with a sandwich before driving down to Ealing.

His plans worked perfectly. Ann invited him in and offered him coffee, as he had hoped.

"I've had to break it to myself that this may be my last visit to this house."

"Do you mean that the mystery is all cleared up?"

"Yes. By this time the murderer of Stella Pomeroy has been arrested."

"Not Casey?"

"No, a man named Burton. But you were right up to a point. Casey had more to do with the case than I thought in the beginning. As a matter of fact, he could have helped us long before this if he had told us all he knew."

Ann listened with wide-open eyes while he related to her the last phases of his investigations.

"How pleased you must be! This solution never occurred to me in my wildest flights. I'm glad that I wasn't entirely wrong about Casey, but I think that Scotland Yard has well earned the reputation it enjoys if all its superintendents are like you."

"Oh, I made mistakes at the beginning just as we all do. The question of the hammer, for instance."

"That was Miles' fault entirely: he practically owned that it was his hammer."

"But we must remember that he wasn't normal that day," said Richardson. "You are glad to have his name entirely cleared, I expect."

"I should think I am, and so will his father and mother be. Won't you come in this evening and let him thank you personally?"

"Thank I will," said Richardson, but his tone was a little flat. Having no further excuse for lingering he took his leave.

His thoughts as he drove back to the police station were not on his recent success. He was recalling some gossip that Mrs Coxon had related to him at their first meeting—gossip which concerned Ann Pomeroy and her cousin. She had told him that Miles Pomeroy's mother had hoped that he would marry Ann, and she had insinuated that Ann herself would not have said no. This, thought Richardson gloomily, is probably what will happen now. They will wait for a decent interval and then... Richardson found this thought more than he could bear.

Of course Ann, with her intelligence and her intuition, was too good for the wife of a bank clerk; too good, also, he owned, for the wife of a detective superintendent. Besides, she had a career before her: she had talked to him about it sometimes over their coffee. No, she would never give up everything to become the wife of an officer in the C.I.D. But Ann did.

THE END

Lightning Source UK Ltd.
Milton Keynes UK
UKOW06f1805190616

276662UK00013B/160/P